UTAH'S BEST POETRY & PROSE 2024

SELECTED WINNERS OF THE OLIVE WOOLLEY BURT AND TYPEWRITER AWARDS

CONTENTS

FOREWORD

It's astounding to me how much quality work comes from the writers of Utah. Right now, you're holding in your hands a pretty good cross-section of that quality and I'm excited for the myriad journeys you get to go on thanks to the magic portal of this book.

Before you embark on this journey, though, I want you to know how hard the work can be.

The writers in this collection toiled endlessly to get into this tome. Every piece in this collection was carefully curated from the winning entries of the annual writing contest held by the League of Utah Writers. The League has been putting some version of this contest on since the 1930s and every year the best and brightest writers of the Beehive state submit their stories and see if the judges smile upon their hard work. As most years, the stories are all judged anonymously and our judges are from out of state, ensuring that there's no bias to their judging. The contest gets hundreds and hundreds of entries, but the winners are usually those that put in the work. Sometimes, you'll find someone who polishes one single story to victory, but you learn by finishing things—at least according to Neil Gaimam—and those that seem to be the most successful and end up writing the award winners are the ones that write so many more pieces. Challenging yourself to work hard enough to enter the contest multiple times has you learning and growing more as a writer with each piece finished. It also gives you even more opportunities to publish because you have more pieces to submit.

I want to call out writers in this collection and pat them on the proverbial back for all the hard work they put in to get here. It means something. There are so many writers in Utah at every level. I'm not sure what it is about this state that allows us to put an emphasis on exploring our creativity like no other place I've seen, but we have it in spades. Maybe it's in the salt water of the great Salt Lake. Or the fresh mountain water from our ample snowpacks—as long as those are going to last. I suppose the most likely issue might be the soupy smog we breathe in the valleys during inversions. Yeah, those long days inside because we don't dare risk our lungs in the car exhaust and industrial pollution could lead to sitting at a desk and dreaming up better worlds.

Makes sense to me.

Whatever the reason is, the stock of writers we have to choose from is an embarrassment of riches at every level. From the hobbyists looking for a private escape and the indie publishers, all the way to the folks at the top of the traditional publishing game, every base is covered inside this collection.

So, to you, dear reader, whether you're a part of the Utah community that produced these stories or not, I hope you can see the breadth of talent that we have among our ranks and in our state. It's a humbling experience to be a part of this group and to watch them soar through their publishing goals and glean the insight from the worlds they create with their worlds. I'm glad you're on this journey with me, and are rewarding their hard work with your attention.

One of Kurt Vonnegut, Jr.'s rules for writing was that you had to use the time of a complete stranger in a way that they won't feel like it's been wasted. I want to assure you that time spent reading this tome will not be time wasted for you. It will show you worlds from past and present, poignant poetry, and soul-baring of the highest calibre. This is as an excellent representation of the writers of Utah have to offer and you're going to enjoy it. So hurry along on your journey and jump on the train before it leaves the station...

It's going to be a wild ride.

Bryan Young
Past President, League of Utah Writers
2023 Writer of the Year
March 2024

THE GOOD GIRL'S CHEMICAL HIGH

M. ROHR

CHRISTMAS. AGE 19.

The smiles seemed a little forced when I entered my aunt's house.

Christmas breakfast was going to be the first time my mother and I had been in the same room with each other since I ran away six months earlier.

Well, according to my mother I ran away.

In my version of events, that fateful day started with my mom warning me that we were going to have a 'chat' when she got home from work. I sat down and sobbed after she left, knowing what that conversation would entail. The prospect of waiting all day to listen to her unleash on me for everything she thought I was doing wrong felt unbearable.

In the midst of my breakdown, I realized I didn't actually have to be there when she got home. I was eighteen. I'd graduated high school just a few days earlier. I had a job. I might have to live in my car, but that seemed phenomenally better than waiting around for another tirade on my failings.

I packed everything I could fit, stayed long enough to tell her when she got home, and left. Fortunately, I was spared from living in my car by an acquaintance from school who was moving in with her grandparents that summer. They had plenty of room and quickly became a second family to me.

When Christmas came around six months later, my family called to invite me. I knew my mom would be there and seeing her would be unpleasant. I wanted to believe my family wanted me there, even if my mom didn't. So, I went.

At the table, I made small talk about my first semester of college with the person sitting next to me while my mom sat at the far end of the table speaking graciously and politely with everyone but me.

An uncle said to me, "You should apologize to your mom."

"Thanks," I said, because I'd tried to explain to him for years what life was like at home, and this was where that conversation went every time.

During clean-up, my mom and my aunt lowered their voices to speak privately. I caught snippets as I helped pass dishes to the kitchen. My mom was clearly venting about all the years she'd worked two and sometimes three jobs to give me a good life, only to have me run away in a fit of 'teenage selfishness.'

I headed to the bathroom. Alone behind the locked door, I pulled out the Oreos I'd brought for just such a moment. I sat on the floor, the familiar anticipation settling over me as I took my first bite. As the first cookie hit my taste buds, a wave of relief swept over me.

Five minutes and a half-dozen cookies later, I cleaned up and returned to the family.

Reinforced and fortified, I stayed for two more hours.

In the rounds of well-wishes before leaving, my aunt gave me a hug and whispered, "Please be kind to your mom. She loves you."

Two blocks from my aunt's house, I pulled my car over and retrieved donuts from the trunk. Then, I leaned my seat back and released the tears I'd been holding as the first bites of sugary fried dough melted in my mouth with a satisfaction that made me want to close my eyes and sigh.

As I finished the first donut, the crying eased. By the end of the second, I was mostly calm. Licking the last of the third from my fingers, I wondered what it would be like to be happy.

I ate a fourth to cheer me up.

Then, finally, the Christmas party now a distant memory, I turned the car on and started back to the home of the family I lived with, contemplating which donut to reward myself with when I got there.

———

When my descent into addiction began, I had no access to cigarettes or hard drugs, alcohol in my home was closely monitored, and I didn't know anyone who would buy it for me. Any adult in my life would have noticed the smells or behaviors associated with cannabis or opiates. Such things—fortunately—weren't options.

Food, however…

Food was the perfect drug: available, socially acceptable, delicious, and the side effects of over-indulgence could be hidden with ease.

And, of course, it was universally available in my home growing up. Even more so as a young adult with a car, a job, and all the freedoms those gave me.

It began with shocking innocence. I was ten when my parents separated, and I discovered eating and watching TV made me not so sad.

By high school, store-bought cookies and other hyperpalatable sweets were my go-to after my mom yelled at me or I felt I'd disappointed her.

By college, I'd catch myself sneaking a fifth piece of cake into my bedroom so I could eat alone. Knowing 'normal' people didn't eat five pieces of cake, I'd convince myself to throw it out. Then

I'd pace, fidget, go a little crazy in the midst of the mental insanity of a craving that I didn't understand or have the skills to cope with, then go back to retrieve the food from the trash because my brain and body were so much calmer if I just ate it.

What started as mild self-soothing in my early teens eventually became my *only* method of self-care. By high school, my solution to anything that upset me became food. Not just eating a meal, but overindulgence on hyperpalatable, sugary foods until I was too ill to move.

Satiety does not apply to food addiction. A food addict loses all sense of hunger and satisfaction. We eat when we need a high, not when we are hungry.

We have a lot in common with smokers, alcoholics, and drug addicts: our drug of choice soothes and distracts from problematic emotions we don't know how to deal with.

Consuming an entire package of Oreos in one sitting does wonders to anesthetize guilt, anger, and stress.

I haven't tried opiates, but I've heard they do the same.

———

I've lost jobs because I caved to a craving an hour before my shift and ended up eating uncontrollably for several hours, too ashamed to call in sick.

I failed college classes because I sat in my car watching others walk to class sipping their coffee or breakfast smoothie while I downed a clearance bakery cake.

But I wasn't obese. I didn't have diabetes. To all who cared to look, I appeared perfectly normal.

And though I didn't feel 'normal,' I also didn't perceive the danger I was in.

Food was necessary, after all. Trying to decline cake or ice cream at family or other social functions attracted protests and offense.

And the high was *nice*.

That fleeting, temporary, utterly satisfying glimpse of physical bliss that relaxed and calmed and made me feel safe and comfortable and *happy*…

It was an elusive, glorious thing.

And convenient.

I could get high on Thanksgiving, in a house full of people, simply by making an "I-shouldn't-but-it's-only-for-today" face and filling another bowl full of brownies or ice cream.

And I didn't regret it. There was nothing in my life that made it so easy to face my mother's displeasure than eating until I was first high and then extremely sick.

The only problem was that some of the time, I didn't *want* to eat so much.

Sometimes, I ate long past self-soothing, spiraling down into a miserable and lasting discomfort accompanied by self-loathing and disgust.

The high didn't feel worth it, afterwards. And on increasingly frequent days, I couldn't seem to stop.

I could put food down, but I'd be so agitated and upset when I walked away that it was only a matter of time until I returned with renewed frenzy to finish off the sugary substance I'd walked away from.

It's a special kind of hell to watch yourself doing something that hurts you and not be able to stop it.

———

As the binge eating became increasingly frequent and uncontrollable, I researched diets and self-help programs.

As I tried and failed in those endeavors, I inevitably ate more. It was easier to *not* try to stop overeating because failing provoked self-loathing that led to eating in order to anesthetize the self-hatred, which led to guilt and shame, which led to more binging.

After one particularly ugly day of uncontrollable eating, I tried purging. There, kneeling in front of the toilet, trying to force myself to vomit, I had my epiphany moment: *I am not okay.*

I checked out books about eating disorders, assuming that was what was wrong. But I wasn't purging routinely, as is typical of bulimia. I wasn't anorexic. I also didn't have a struggle with body image, as the texts seemed to suggest was a fundamental symptom in both disorders.

One symptom did apply: abusing or restricting food in relation to emotional distress, which, the texts suggested, might be treated with counseling.

The first counselor told me that every day after work he got one of his favorite chocolates from the cabinet above the fridge and ate it while he looked at his garden. He suggested that food routines such as this could be extremely helpful for people with eating disorders. So, I went home and made my favorite cookies, planning to eat one every day. Then I fidgeted and paced, eventually dissolving into hysterical crying, unable to think of anything except how much I *needed* those cookies.

The next thing I knew, I was in my room, alone, sitting on the floor scarfing down two at a time. I had no memory of retrieving the cookie dish. And I was *furious* someone had suggested I limit my ingestion of such sweet, lovely, happy cookies.

The second counselor gave me a copy of *Intuitive Eating* and explained that sometimes people place so many restrictions on food that they need to release all of those restrictions in order to start the healing process.

I tried that, too. I ate everything and anything. No guilt trips. No arguments. No internal battles. I gained thirty pounds in three months and lost my job because I was so physically ill all the time I couldn't get to work.

When the uncontrollable urges to eat didn't ease, I found a third counselor. After six weeks, she told me I seemed to be doing very well, and perhaps I should only come see her once a month.

I didn't tell her I couldn't hardly stand up because I was in so much pain after my most recent binge. Instead, I smiled, thanked her for her help, and never went back to see her again.

The continued failures to achieve any success through counseling left me with the lasting impression that I was too broken for mental health experts. If I couldn't fix me, and professionals couldn't fix me, it seemed obvious nothing else could fix me, either.

———

In my mid-twenties, I went to the last friend I had left: an adult child in my second family. I'd lost touch with any friends I'd made in school, either high school or college, because I was so humiliated and disturbed by the increasing frequency of the binge eating.

I told that one friend I thought I had an eating disorder.

The next day, he gave me a hefty stack of literature on prayer and God's power to heal.

I read it.

Then, as some Christians do, I added fasting to my prayer practice.

I lost twenty pounds in two months of fasting before I gave up and started eating again, this time with a renewed vigor I hadn't thought possible.

The friend I'd told about the eating disorder told his family what I'd said.

I overheard them talking about me.

One of them said, "I wish I could tell her she's better than this, to just get over it."

In hindsight, I realize that with great familial love, a person who cared dearly for me was venting frustration that something so seemingly simple might be handicapping my happiness and potential.

At the time, the hurt felt irreparable, and I started packing to move out.

Self-help books frequently share stories of people whose bad habits stopped being a problem once they moved or changed jobs or took a long vacation. I hoped moving would be that solution for me.

It wasn't.

I quickly discovered that renting a room in a house of college girls meant I didn't have the same need to hide my uncontrollable eating as I'd had while living with my second family. In the new place, no one noticed if I took a pizza and three milkshakes to my room. If they did, they didn't care.

That was fine with me. Liberating, actually.

I could get high any time I wanted.

And I did.

———

A year after moving away from my second family, I spent an entire week in my room eating, not leaving except to get more edible substances and use the bathroom.

Sick and disgusted and at a loss, I looked around for anything or anyone else who might help. I found nothing. I didn't talk to co-workers outside of work and didn't feel a close connection with any of them. I knew names of people in my college classes but had no interaction with them outside of the classroom. At church, I arrived late and left early in order to avoid exposing my shameful secret in any way. The hurt I'd felt after the reactions by my second family still stung bitterly. In my mind, counseling had been tried and proved useless.

In desperation, I went to the last person in the world who—in my mind—might have an interest in my well-being and obligation to help save me from my hell.

"I think I have an eating disorder," I said.

My mother frowned. "What makes you *think* you have an eating disorder?"

The emphasis on the word "think" bothered me.

Before I could get past that, she said, "You don't need to look like women on TV, you know. That's not normal or healthy."

It seemed so obvious to me that this had nothing—*nothing*—to do with the stereotypical misunderstandings of anorexia and bulimia that I had no response. I hadn't considered how I would describe the problem. I wasn't going to tell anyone that sometimes I came to after a binge only to find myself lying on my bedroom floor next to empty food packages having no memory of eating them.

I was so ashamed of it that I couldn't describe the symptoms. Couldn't even begin to formulate a sentence that would describe my hell.

"How's school?" my mom asked, changing the subject to bring our dinner conversation back to something more 'normal.'

Grateful for the change of topic, I told her about my classes and then spun an acceptable tale about the social events I'd attended.

I hadn't actually gone to any social events. I'd get twitchy and agitated in any situation involving food. Like the proverbial "little kid in a candy store" insanity but on steroids and laced with the paranoid rapidity characteristic of a cocaine addict in need of a hit.

So instead of socializing, I sat in my bedroom, alone, and ate.

Well, not *alone*.

I had my food with me.

———

A recovering alcoholic once described alcohol as her soul mate. That's exactly how I felt about food.

In my mind, I'd tried every option I had: counseling, telling a friend, and then my second family, and, finally, trying to talk to my mom about it.

I stopped trying to fix whatever it was that was wrong with me and surrendered—utterly and completely. Life became nothing more than a calculation between the previous binge and how long it would be until I got my next one. There was no joy or happiness or laughter unless it was with food. No sadness or sorrow unless it was a lack of food.

While my days spiraled into a roller coaster of emotion based on how long it had been since my previous high and how long I had to wait until I could get my next, I got nearly straight A's and paid my way through college. I paid my own bills, went to church, helped elderly neighbors, and made appropriate appearances at family events.

None of it meant anything.

It was like watching someone else live my life—the conversations I had, the people I interacted with—all of it was someone else using my body to go through the necessary motions. Meaning only existed when I ate.

My highs were my lovers and my friends.

When I was lonely, I found companionship in food. When I was sad, solace came only from eating.

No one understood my misery—except food. No shared happiness with me—except food.

Food calmed the madness, the guilt, the shame. It took away the pain.

Food didn't judge me. Didn't tell me I should be better. Didn't tell me to stop trying to be something I wasn't. Food was kind, gentle, and understanding. Food didn't hurt my feelings. Food stayed with me when I felt lonely. Food was never too busy or distracted. Food gave me its undivided attention. Food provided devoted affection.

It was, as that woman described, the perfect soul mate.

———

In church one day, a woman shared her experience overcoming an addiction to opiates. At its worst, her life had been nothing but a calculation between how long since the last high and how long until the next. Nothing else existed. She maintained a marriage, took care of three kids, worked part time, participated in community service... all the while caring about absolutely nothing except when she could take her next pill.

That was *me.*

The years of isolation shattered. I wasn't having a mental breakdown. I wasn't unfixable. Eating disorder treatments hadn't helped because I didn't have an eating disorder.

I was an addict.

I found that woman after the service and started sobbing before I could even say hello.

She wrapped her arms around me and whispered, "I know, sweetheart. I know."

———

Three days later, I drove nearly forty minutes from home to ensure no one recognized me when I attended my first recovery meeting. The woman from church had invited me to her meeting, but I'd declined. I didn't even want to be in the same space as anyone familiar for this first meeting.

A quick survey of the half dozen people in the semi-circle led me to sit between a small, timid looking man probably in his early fifties, and a soccer mom in knee-length shorts sporting light makeup and a ponytail.

The meeting started. The facilitators introduced themselves and explained the meeting format and told me I could say "pass" if I didn't want to participate.

The soccer mom to my left shared about a decade of shooting heroin into her veins between her kids' sports and music practices. Her husband didn't know. Her family thought she was meeting with a book club.

Next, the man to my right shared about nearly forty years fighting the addiction that brought him recovery. Based on a few of his vague comments, I quickly realized I was sitting next to a person who had, in the throes of sexual addiction, committed heinous crimes.

The facilitators asked me if I'd like to share.

Yeah, right.

What would I say?

"Hi, I eat cookies."

No f***ing way.

Those people had *serious* challenges. I just needed to stop eating so much.

I left the meeting promising myself I'd never overeat again.

That week was a brutal awakening as I paid attention, for the first time in years, to what my daily life consisted of.

Every day that week, I woke up sick and miserable from the previous days' binge and knew that within hours I'd be watching myself eat until I was in physical and emotional agony. I couldn't stop it. I hated it. I hated myself. I hated every second I was alive.

"Dear God," I thought, reciting the only prayer I had left, "please don't make me live another day."

I bought ice cream on my way to the meeting the following week.

The next week, I did the same.

———

After nearly six months of sitting quietly in those recovery meetings, I overcame the embarrassment of introducing myself to 'real' addicts.

"Would you like to share this week?" asked the woman leading the meeting.

"Hi," I said. "I'm an addict. I… have an eating disorder."

"Welcome," the group said in unison, as is the 12-step custom.

No one laughed when I said eating disorder.

After the meeting, the facilitator told me her daughter had a similar struggle. It started when her parents divorced, and she began eating her feelings because she didn't know how to cope with them. The facilitator gave me her phone number and invited me to call so we could chat one-on-one.

For the first time in years, the chasm between me and the outside world had been bridged. Someone *knew* me. Knew what was wrong. Didn't despise me because of it.

As we walked out, the facilitator told me the title of a book her daughter had found helpful. "It was the best we found on food addiction," she said.

Food addiction.

Finally—*finally*—my nightmare had a name.

I cried all the way home.

———

Food is sometimes referred to as a good girl's chemical high. The name is not just apt but quite perfect.

Drugs weren't available to me, but hyperpalatable foods, particularly sugary ones, provided a sensory experience leading to a dopamine response which numbed difficult emotions. The relief became a high. A cue-reward cycle began. I became dependent.

Part of the tragedy of the last twenty years is how different they might have been if I'd latched on to alcohol or cigarettes or prescription painkillers instead of food. I can't help but assume my attempts to ask for help would have had very different outcomes.

With that in mind, I've worked hard to find the courage to share a little of my experience with people in my church congregation, with ecclesiastical leaders, with twelve-step meetings, and with friends who are parents.

"If you're the kind of parent who talks to your kids about drugs," I tell them, "then talk to them about food, too."

As with any compulsive substance or behavior, early awareness is key.

Several times, after speaking with groups about my experience with addiction and recovery, someone has come up to me afterwards, crying so hard they can't introduce themselves or explain.

Like the woman so many years ago did for me, I hug them as tight as I possibly can, tell them I understand, and ask if they'll come to a meeting.

———

CHRISTMAS. AGE 37.

My husband, kids, and I arrive as breakfast is set out. I make the rounds giving hugs, then make my way to the kitchen where I find a small space for the crockpot I brought with a favorite dish of mine. It's a crockpot chocolate cake made with avocados, almond flour, and honey. Yes, I'm planning to eat chocolate cake for Christmas breakfast. It's sweet and I think of it as a treat, but there's nothing in it that is addictive to me.

I started preparing myself for this day almost two months ago. Around the middle of October, I stopped anything that could be stopped: work projects, house projects, self-improvement projects, homemaking projects. I emailed all the distant relatives, told them happy holidays, then gave myself permission to not answer calls, emails, or texts until January.

We've been eating off disposable dishes for nearly a week to minimize kitchen clean-up. I made freezer meals, too, so I wouldn't have to cook for most of December. I purchased extra linens and kids' clothes from a thrift store so that we can simply toss the used stuff in the laundry room and pull out clean ones. I'll deal with it in January.

This is my self-care bubble.

Most importantly, any edible substance in my house that might possibly be problematic for me over the holidays was either discarded or given away.

Over the course of Christmas morning, some in my extended family ask why I'm not eating the toxic substances they've brought. I give vague but firm answers about dietary preferences. I've practiced those responses in front of a mirror.

I sit as far away from the buffet as I can. I try not to look at it. I get agitated because I know it's there. I take long breaks in the bathroom—*without* edible substances—for deep breathing and centering.

After two hours, I give my husband the signal that I can't be here anymore.

When we get in the car, I close my eyes and cry—whether from relief at success or misery at leaving behind that buffet of sweet and intoxicating bliss, I'm not sure.

Right now, it doesn't matter.

I did what I'd set out to do: my first Christmas sober in more than twenty years.

HART AND SOUL

SEPTEMBER ROBERTS

RYAN

Ryan checked his watch. Again. The line backed up to the door, and no one seemed to care but him. What was it with these people? Why did they have to talk so much?

The Hart and Soul Café offered a variety of food, but it was their coffee that stood out. And only two people separated him from the thing he wanted most: the darkest, richest coffee in Salt Lake City. He wanted to push his way to the front so he could get on with his day, but he resisted the urge and waited like the model citizen that he was.

The man in front of him stepped forward.

"What can I get you?" the woman behind the counter asked, just like she asked everyone.

"I don't know, Morgan. What do I *need* today?"

The woman, Morgan, leaned forward, grasped the man's hands, and beamed at him. There was something radiant about the way she looked at him. She never looked at Ryan like that.

She closed her eyes for a moment and nodded. "You need a blueberry muffin and a cup of Earl Grey."

The man bobbed his head up and down like she had just suggested something life altering.

"It's just tea and a muffin," Ryan mumbled. Maybe if he said it louder, he could break the spell between this poor sap and the woman.

Before the man left the counter, he took a big bite of muffin and sighed. "How do you always know?"

The woman's smile grew. "It's a gift," she said with a wink.

Honestly, who winks?

The man finally moved out of the way, and Ryan stepped up. He opened his mouth to order, but the woman spoke first, her radiant smile turning down a few notches.

"Coffee, black," she said in a deep voice that sounded like an approximation of his.

He snapped his mouth closed and nodded.

While she prepared his coffee, she said, "A little coconut oil would add so much flavor."

He opened his mouth to respond, but she went on.

"But you don't want that. Or cream. Or butter from grass-fed cows. Or, heaven forbid, sugar." She turned and placed his cup on the counter in front of him. "Just coffee. Black." She gave him a smile, but it was tight.

"Yes." He held out his credit card and waited for her to take it. Instead, she took his hand in hers. Even though he'd seen her interact with other customers like this, it was the first time she'd touched him.

Her glowing smile returned, the soft lines around her eyes deepening. "You need a lemon poppyseed muffin."

For some inexplicable reason, he didn't pull away. Instead, he smiled and leaned forward, drawn to her like a meteoroid drawn to Earth. Wait a minute. This is how she did it. She blinded her customers with that smile and got them to buy all sorts of fattening treats. Not today, Satan.

"No, thank you." When he removed his hand from hers, he left his credit card behind.

"Are you sure?" She narrowed her eyes as the smile dimmed again. "It'll make you happy."

Going to the gym made him happy. Getting to work early made him happy. Eating a muffin would not, in fact, make him happy. "No, thank you."

MORGAN

As Morgan swept the café that evening, she couldn't shake the unsettling feeling she'd had since that morning. Since she'd spoken with Coffee, Black. Or, more accurately, since she'd looked into his face and noticed how handsome he was. Why was it that men aged so well? The gray at his temples made him look distinguished. The gray in her hair made her look like Broom Hilda.

He came every day at the same time and always only ordered coffee. She had loads of regulars, and they were all friendly. Except him.

There she was, dispensing happiness with every bite and Coffee, Black didn't want any of it. If people knew the truth behind her gift, they would be lining up around the block. The Hart women had to be careful when it came to how they used their magic and who knew about it. Her grandmother had made the mistake of letting the wrong people find out and spent most of her life trying to meet the extreme demands of the rich and eccentric. Turns out, some people aren't happy no matter what you give them. It was one of many cautionary tales told in her family.

When she had touched him that morning, she knew exactly what he needed. The last time he'd had a lemon poppyseed muffin was when he was sitting in his grandmother's kitchen on a bright spring morning. Remembering it now made her smile as she emptied the dustpan. Sometimes, the flashes of the past were so strong she got all wrapped up in them. That one had been warm and lovely, and she wanted to burrow deep into it. She wanted to show him that remembering those wonderful moments would make him happy as well.

Why couldn't she stop thinking about how attractive he looked when he smiled? It made her all warm and squishy inside. It was best he didn't experience joy around her. She didn't know what would happen if he smiled at her again. She probably wouldn't survive it.

She'd been practicing her gift her entire life. Her mother had shown her how to focus on the light, never the dark. So, she honed her skills, dipped into the brightest, happiest memories, and helped people reconnect with them. She loved food, and she loved making people happy. Win-win.

Except Coffee, Black. She couldn't win with him.

RYAN

Over the next few days, Ryan watched Morgan closely. He thought about the smile on her face more than was probably healthy, as if the way she'd touched his hand had knocked something loose in his brain. On Friday, he waited for three entire minutes while a woman cried over her scone. He rolled his eyes and sighed.

"Thank you, Morgan," she finally said, wiping her eyes.

Morgan. The smiling, coffee-making, hand-holding woman.

The two women hugged, and a pang of jealousy hit him. The hug looked so intimate and warm.

Jealousy? Where had that come from? What did he have to be jealous of? He was fine.

The fact that he couldn't remember the last time someone had hugged him didn't mean anything. Wait. He knew. Five years ago, his mom had wrapped her arms around his waist and squeezed while the open casket holding his grandmother stood a few feet away.

"Ryan?"

They had gotten her makeup wrong. She never wore that much blush.

"Ryan?" His mom said his name softer, her voice closer now. No, not his mom. Morgan.

Pulled out of the worst memory of his life, he focused on Morgan where she stood in front of him, her hand on his, a sad smile on her beautiful face. His sorrow threatened to swallow him whole, overwhelming everything else. Jealousy and impatience forgotten, Ryan let Morgan guide him away from the counter.

"Have a seat. I'll get your coffee for you." She led him to a table and let go of him.

He looked down at his hand and blinked. For some reason, he missed the warmth of her touch. It was the first time he'd sat in one of the café chairs, and he wondered why he hadn't done it before. The longer he sat there, the more he thought about his grandmother. This café smelled like her house. No wonder he'd been thinking about her so much.

"This will make you happy." She placed a bag on the table next to his usual cup of coffee. "On the house." She patted his hand gently and walked away.

Happy? How could he be happy when the memories of his grandmother's death held on to him so tightly? He inhaled deeply and closed his eyes. Inhale, hold, exhale, hold. Repeat. Just like his therapist showed him. It took a while before he felt like himself again. The ache in his chest was more manageable.

With his coffee and treat in one hand and his briefcase in the other, he walked to work. In all the years he'd been at the insurance agency, it was the first day he arrived late. The day was full of firsts.

He sat at his desk and stared at his computer screen, then at the bag Morgan had given him with his coffee. He expected to find a lemon poppyseed muffin, but to his surprise, he found a cranberry orange scone.

Would it be as good as the last ones he'd had with his grandmother? Should he eat it to find out? Morgan would ask him how it was the next time he got his morning coffee. If he didn't eat it, he'd have to explain himself. That would take forever. Better to eat it and prove that a scone wouldn't make him happy.

He'd never been so wrong in all his life.

MORGAN

Ryan had been on Morgan's mind all day. Again. That morning, despite her years of homing in on people's happiness, she couldn't avoid the grief spilling out of him. It had taken her a full minute to find a bright memory, something strong enough to balance him. And the two memories stayed with her all day. Light and dark. Joy and sorrow.

She flipped the last chair onto the table when the bell over the door chimed. Oops. She had forgotten to lock up again.

"We're closed," she called out as she turned. "Oh, it's you."

Ryan stood stiffly, his hand gripping his briefcase.

"Ryan? Are you okay?"

He tilted his head. "How do you know my name?"

"It's on your credit card, which I have seen every workday for the last year." She didn't mention why today had been the first day she'd used his real name. She felt connected to him now. He didn't need to know that she only called her friends by their names. Friends and customers were the same thing, right? "Can I get you something?"

"No. I'm sorry. I'll let you finish closing for the night." He turned to go, then stopped and added, "Thank you for earlier." His lip twitched in one corner. "You were right. That scone did make me happy."

"Oh?" She repressed a grin, but it was a hard thing.

"My grandmother was a fantastic baker. The day I graduated from college, she taught me how to make my favorite food in the whole world: cranberry orange scones." His mouth tipped up on both sides now. "We squeezed fresh oranges to make the glaze." He chuckled and closed his eyes, and when he looked at her again, they were full of happy tears. "We ate all of them and licked the pan afterward."

She had been right. She couldn't survive this man, smiling at her with his slightly crooked teeth and lips that looked so soft. "That sounds wonderful."

"It was." He sighed. "I miss her, and today, I got to be with her again. Thank you for that."

Moments like this made the loneliness of her life worthwhile. "Any time."

"For the record, your scones are just as good as hers."

RYAN

Monday morning, Ryan showed up a few minutes early to get his coffee. He'd spent the whole weekend thinking about his encounter with Morgan. The way she'd soothed him with her touch and reminded him of one of the happiest memories of his grandmother just when he needed it most.

He'd gone to live with his grandmother after high school, escaping his small South Carolina town and getting to know someone who loved him more than he thought possible. Those years had been the happiest of his life, which was probably why he still lived in Salt Lake City.

He needed to see if Morgan could do it again. It had absolutely nothing to do with the way she made his heart beat just a little faster or how adorable she looked with a bit of flour on her cheek. Not at all. This was all part of an experiment. If she could pick another food that made him happy, then he had to admit all these people were on to something. How could one person change his perspective so effortlessly with one bite? His usual impatience morphed into curiosity. Yep, just curiosity.

When it was his turn, he stepped up to the counter and basked in the warmth of her smile. It didn't matter if he believed she could magically pick the right food for each person. He couldn't help smiling back. Why had he spent the last year resisting her? His life was infinitely better when Morgan smiled at him.

"Nice to see you, Ryan."

"Hi, Morgan."

She narrowed her eyes. "How do you know *my* name?"

Heat flushed his cheeks. "I heard someone use it. I wasn't trying to eavesdrop. I just—"

"I'm messing with you. Everyone knows my name." Her shoulders shook with laughter. "Coffee, black. Right?"

"And?" he added quietly.

She raised her eyebrows as her smile grew. "And?"

"I was hoping you would tell me what I need," he whispered as he reached out to her, feeling ridiculous.

But she didn't hesitate to hold his hand in hers. If he was honest with himself, he would have to admit that getting to touch her was the highlight of this experiment. Within a few seconds, she said, "Today, you need a slice of spinach and cheese quiche."

Ryan typically skipped breakfast, but he barely made it to his desk before the urge to eat it overpowered him. The first bite took him back to a brunch he'd had with his parents at their favorite restaurant. His mom had let him have a sip of her mimosa, and he'd felt like a grown-up, even though he'd only been ten.

Morgan suggested something different every day for the next week. And each time, he smiled and laughed while he ate the food she'd made. There was something special about her. He didn't know how she did it, but it wasn't a fluke. No one could be right that often, and based on her dedicated clientele, she was right one hundred percent of the time. He'd seen enough to believe in her gift, as she called it. The experiment was over. Now he had to thank her with more than words.

He left work early again to stop by the café but found the door locked this time. Morgan swept her way around the tables, her hair falling across her forehead. He almost turned to leave when their eyes met, and a smile spread across her face.

She unlatched the door and invited him in. "Hi, Ryan."

"Hi, Morgan." His heart picked up, just like it did every time he interacted with her lately. "Do you need any help?"

"With what?"

"You tell me. I wanted to thank you for all the happy moments you've given me, and the only thing I can offer is my time, so put me to work. If you're comfortable with me being here, that is. With you. I mean, just us." What was it about her that made him blush and fall over his words?

"I'm very comfortable with you." Was she blushing too? That was too much to hope for.

MORGAN

Morgan beamed. She showed her love and appreciation by helping others, so the offer squeezed her heart. How had she ever thought she couldn't win with Ryan? "I still need to cash out, take care of the trash, and prep ingredients for tomorrow."

Ryan placed his briefcase on the table by the door. Then, he removed his suit jacket, folded it neatly, and rolled up his sleeves, showing off his strong forearms. "I'll finish sweeping, then take out the trash."

"Thank you."

"No," he said, taking the broom out of her hands. "*I'm* thanking *you*."

She nodded and stepped into the kitchen, pressing a damp rag against her cheeks to cool them down. When she had things well in hand, she picked up a spare apron and brought it out to him. "You should protect your …" She stopped and stared at him squatting over the dustpan. When had he loosened his tie and undone the top button of his shirt? "Clothes," she finished and averted her eyes as he stood. She should definitely *not* be watching the way his strong thighs flexed against his slacks.

"My hands are kind of full. Can you help?" He lifted his arms and turned around, presenting an even better view.

Morgan stepped up behind him and wrapped the apron with

her café's name around his waist. Thank goodness it wasn't the kind that went around his neck. That would mean his face would be close. Close enough to kiss. She needed to stop all those thoughts. He was being nice. She was being inappropriate. Before she could think about how nice he smelled or how warm his back was through his clothes, she tied a bow in the strings and took four steps backward. "I'll be in the kitchen."

She'd been compiling a list of recipes to make the following day, so she set to work gathering supplies and ingredients. It made mornings more manageable.

"What are you making tomorrow?"

Morgan squeaked in surprise and put her hand over her heart. "I forgot you were here."

Ryan grimaced. "I didn't mean to scare you."

"It's okay. Not your fault. I was in my own head. That's how it always is when I'm planning the menu."

"How do you decide? Do your customers tell you what they want?"

"Something like that." It took a special kind of balancing act to anticipate what customers would need from day to day, even with her gift. "Blueberry lemon scones, bacon and cheese frittata, double chocolate muffins." She paused and thought back to the memory she'd glimpsed that morning when she'd touched his hand. "And cinnamon coffee cake."

"With a streusel topping?" His eyes went wide.

"Obviously." She grinned, and he reciprocated. When had he started to smile at her like that?

"I've never had your coffee cake before."

"I hope you'll like it."

"I like everything you make." A beautiful rosy flush spread across Ryan's cheeks. He cleared his throat and nodded at the garbage. "I already took care of the can under the register and by the door. Is this the last one?"

"Yes, thank you."

By the time she finished kitchen prep, Ryan had removed his

apron and shrugged back into his jacket. "Thank you for letting me help. Can I come again tomorrow?"

"You don't have to."

"I want to." The smile on his lips was so sweet.

"Then yes, please come again tomorrow."

RYAN

The clock on Ryan's desk ticked down the hours until he could see Morgan again. Usually, he'd get so wrapped up in work that he didn't bother to leave until hunger forced him home. But now, he took shorter lunches and didn't take on extra cases so he could leave early to see her. He'd finished the last bite of his cinnamon coffee cake an hour ago, managing to savor it all day long as he went through house insurance claims. There was always at least one thing in her pastry case that he loved. Sometimes it felt like she baked just for him.

At five o'clock sharp, he stepped through the doors of the café. "It's me," he called out.

Morgan's voice came from the kitchen, "Be right out. Will you lock the door and come grab your apron?"

His apron. He liked the sound of that. He liked it even more when she put his apron on him, but he couldn't think of an excuse why he might need her help again, so he put it on himself.

They moved together just like they had the previous night, like they'd been doing it their whole lives. Like he could continue to do this for the rest of his life.

The realization slapped him upside the head, stopping him in his tracks. Until recently, he worked until seven or eight each night. But work didn't make him happy, not like this. Then again, how could denying homeowners coverage make anyone happy? Morgan had shown him how to find joy in simple things, and it changed the way he looked at his life.

"Are you okay?" Morgan frowned from her position behind the register.

"Yeah, just thinking about work." He liked feeling useful and being praised by his boss, but the actual work didn't fulfill him, and if he was honest, it never had. "How long have you been in business?"

"Fifteen years overall. Five at this location."

He whistled. "Does it make you happy?"

Morgan smiled and nodded. "I make people happy every day."

"Sure, but does it make *you* happy?" When she narrowed her eyes, he went on. "I make my boss happy every day, but I think I hate my job."

"Oh, Ryan." The tenderness in her voice nearly broke him.

"I know, right? I just realized that. But what about you?" The thought of her going through the motions made him want to set the world on fire. When had those feelings started?

She sighed and seemed to really think about it. "I do. It's a lot of work, and my mornings are very early, but it's satisfying. When I see the look on someone's face after they've taken a bite of a muffin, it makes it all worth it."

"It makes *what* worth it?"

Morgan shrugged. "The loneliness. I never made time for more, and I'm just realizing that maybe I'm missing out."

"My grandmother warned me about that. She told me there were more important things in life than work. I never believed her." The addition of 'until now' didn't need to be said.

"She was a wise woman."

Ryan nodded. "She would've loved you. You're exactly—" He cut himself off just in time. He had been about to say that she was the kind of woman his grandmother wanted him to marry. Someone kind, funny, and warm. The kind of woman Ryan had stopped looking for years ago because she didn't exist. Except apparently, she did.

MORGAN

"I'm exactly what?" Morgan said, wishing she could read his mind. She could practically see his brain short-circuiting.

"Like her. I was going to say you're just like her." That was definitely *not* what he was going to say, but she would let him off the hook this time.

Morgan laughed. "You only say that because my scones are as good as hers."

Ryan grinned, and the brightness of it knocked the air out of her lungs. "Don't let it go to your head."

"Too late. I'm going to be insufferable from now on." When their laughter quieted, she smiled at him. "Thanks for keeping me company. It's been really nice. And the help. I really appreciate all the work you're doing here."

"So, I can keep coming?"

Forever. She hoped he kept coming forever. "Yes, please."

———

True to his word, Ryan showed up promptly at five. Morgan looked forward to it more than any other part of her day—except maybe in the mornings when she got to touch him for a few seconds to find what he needed.

The temptation to ask him out became stronger each time they interacted, but the idea of him rejecting her was too much to handle. What if it made him uncomfortable? What if he stopped coming? Or worse, what if they went on a date and things went well? Eventually, he'd find out about her family, and it would be too much. She would scare him away, just like her last boyfriend. She had to tell him everything. If he stayed, maybe she'd get up the courage to ask him out.

With her heart in her throat, she watched the door from the coziest table in the café and waited.

At five, he stepped inside, locked the door, and was halfway through rolling up his sleeves when he finally looked at her. "What's wrong?"

"We need to talk." Seeing the panic on his face, she quickly added, "About my family." She gestured to the seat across from her.

Traces of panic remained, but curiosity overpowered everything else on his face. "I'm listening."

"I need you to keep what I'm about to tell you to yourself."

"I promise," he said without hesitation.

She swallowed hard and hoped she wasn't making a mistake. "My family is… special."

A wide smile turned up his mouth. "Of course, it is. You're a part of it."

The compliment, paired with his smile, made her stomach flip. But she had to stay focused. To just get it out. She shook her head. "By special, I mean magic. We're witches." She had a family of personal shoppers, bartenders, and cooks. "We have the gift of happiness. Mine is linked to food."

"Magic food." He tilted his head.

"Not really. The food isn't magic. It's your connection to it that matters."

Ryan's eyes widened. "That's how you know. Every day for weeks now. You know exactly what to feed me."

"When I take a person's hand—" she reached out to him, and he placed his hand in hers without hesitation, "—I can sort through their memories. They shine like bright lights." She'd noticed his changing over the last few weeks. Instead of being singular memories, they were layered. Cranberry orange scones were tied to his grandmother and her now. She closed her eyes and focused. "I see snapshots of joy in your life. Sharing spaghetti with your cat when you were six. Dipping fries in a shake on a date in college." She laughed. "Your date thought you were weird."

He chuckled. "She did. My grandmother told me she wasn't worth my time. You can see all that?"

"I can." She hesitated to open her eyes, terrified of what she would find, but finally looked at him.

Ryan had wonder in his eyes. "You're magic."

"I am."

"You're a witch."

"A *good* witch," she emphasized.

"Witches exist."

Morgan nodded. "We do, and I trust you to keep that to yourself."

"I'll keep your secret." He rubbed his thumb against her palm. "Thank you for trusting me."

"Thank you for not freaking out." She laughed nervously. "That could've gone horribly. Believe me."

He frowned. "You've told someone before."

"Yes. And he didn't stick around for long after."

"That's why you're lonely."

"Yes." She hadn't opened up to anyone in years. It had always been safer to keep her secrets and accept that the joy in her life came through her customers. But Ryan changed everything.

"Why me? Why now?" His cheeks flushed.

"Because I like you, and I want to spend more time with you. And, before I ask the question I've been wanting to ask, I didn't want any secrets between us."

He leaned forward, closing the distance between them. "I don't have any secrets to share, so I think we're in the clear now. What's your question?"

Her mouth went dry, and it became nearly impossible to focus on anything other than his lips and the way his chest rose and fell just as quickly as hers. "Will you have dinner with me?"

"Obviously, yes." He smiled. "I have a question for you, too."

He said yes. To her. To a *date* with her. She wanted to sing and dance around the room, but that would have to wait. "What?"

"Can I kiss you?"

Stupefied, she nodded and leaned closer to him. When their lips met, a sigh escaped her throat. She'd been thinking about kissing this man for weeks now, and it was better than she dreamed it could be. Soft, sweet, and just demanding enough to let her know he wanted her just as much as she wanted him.

Ryan leaned back and let out a slow breath. "Are you sure you're not a magic kisser?"

Morgan laughed and squeezed his hand. "I don't think so, but we might have to try it again to check. First, dinner."

As if on cue, his stomach growled. "Where are we going?"

"To my favorite Indian place."

He stood and pulled her to her feet. "I've never had Indian food before."

Morgan grinned up at him. "I know. Tonight, you'll make a new memory. One that's just for us."

THE PASTOR'S WIFE

MEG CONDIE

She was thinking about donuts when he climaxed. About the two decades since her last honest donut. About the single donut she'd secretly indulged in each year on their wedding anniversary.

His final grunt of satisfaction reminded her of that sweet sigh of relief she uttered after taking her first bite of last year's donut. It had been a cake donut—her favorite. The bear claw from the year before left her a little disappointed, but it had been so long since she'd had one that she'd wanted to try it in case her tastes had changed. The glazed donut the year before that had come from a little mom and pop shop where they still used the original recipe from great-grandma.

She thought she'd probably go there tomorrow for this year's anniversary donut. If she only broke his rules about consumerism and mass market goods once a year, it was going to be the best donut the tri-county area could produce.

Her husband drew back and fell onto the mattress beside her, reminding her she'd forgotten about him.

She pulled the blanket up the way he liked, but he sat up, pushing the blanket down and swinging his feet off the side of the bed. "I need to get going."

"I'll get you a sandwich to take with you," she said.

"The volunteer lunch is today."

Meaning he didn't need a sandwich. Also meaning she had a busy day ahead of her.

She made the bed as he headed for the shower. Retrieving her robe, she headed downstairs to start the casseroles for the luncheon.

———

Four hours later she was showered and dressed, six casseroles dispatched to the church luncheon, the next six thawing in the kitchen window while the aroma of baking bread filled the house.

Laundry started. Bathroom wiped down. Casseroles in progress. First batch of rolls baking. Second rising. Coffee warming for any of her husband's parishioners who came by.

With a sigh, she paused at the kitchen window, smelling the bitterness of the cheap bulk coffee beans roasting and imaging the lush brew she'd indulge in tomorrow.

Anniversary day was tomorrow.

It had started innocently. The day before they'd married, he'd gone to sell his car, which was his commitment to ridding himself of worldly goods and embarking on a charitable life.

While he was gone, she'd bought a dozen donuts. By the time he got back, not just the donuts but the evidence of them was gone.

Twenty years—and twenty secret donut anniversaries—later, she had to ask if this Christian simplicity lifestyle was worth it. What, *exactly*, had she done in the last two decades to make the world a better place?

As if the universe were answering, her eyes fell on the thrift-store hutch lined with tokens acknowledging her husband's work that they'd collected since they'd married. Mission trips to Central America to build houses and wells and plumbing. A year in the Congo building schools and training teachers. Two trips to India to work on clean water projects. Newspaper articles, online write-ups, charitable awards. An entire wall celebrating his work.

He, in all his devotion and single-minded focus on casting off worldliness and doing God's work, didn't even indulge in the sin of store-bought donuts.

And her…?

She cooked and cleaned and did laundry to support him and his charitable work—a perfect façade of piety and abstinence and devotion to hide a growing sense of disappointment and resentment.

The doorbell rang, interrupting those inappropriate thoughts.

It was Mrs. Henwick, most likely, returning to see if the bread was ready to take over to the church for the luncheon.

Instead of the gray and papery Mrs. Henwick, Andrea Jones stood with a box of donuts and two hot to-go cups with a local coffee shop logo.

"Can you believe this?" Andrea offered an impressive eye roll while juggling the donuts and coffee—a tattered copy of *Middlemarch* sat propped between the cups.

The women's group had been trying to find an assignment in the congregation that suited Andrea's "bold" personality. Six months ago, they'd asked Andrea to organize the book club meetings. For some unknown reason, Andrea had thrived. She prepared surveys to determine which books the club should read and baked at least three kinds of muffins for each month's meeting.

"Excuse me?" the pastor's wife asked.

"Sorry, Mrs. B. This *book*. This godforsaken book." Andrea stepped into the house. "Can you believe people read this? In schools? This is what's wrong with education." She toed off her sandals, the donuts almost tipping over as she lost her balance in the process. She hurried to catch the food but not the book, letting it drop to the floor next to her shoes. "And Old Mrs. J adores it, and Emily—Grumpy Emily, not New Emily—said it would 'inspire us to higher devotion.' Ugh! Do they not know that feminism happened? Then, Mrs. Henwick said it's your favorite and that she reads it every year in order to appreciate your many sacrifices…blah, blah, blah."

The pastor's wife closed the door behind Andrea.

She liked Andrea. Had liked her since she'd first visited Sunday services a year ago and announced during a lesson on Noah and the Ark that she didn't think God should favor white evangelicals like that.

Andrea kicked the book from the tile entry where it had fallen, sending it sliding across the carpet to the living room. "And I said to Mrs. Peterson—the nosy Mrs. P, not the redhaired Mrs. P—that there's *no way* I'm reading this nonsense. And she turned up her nose at me—for real. Up it went like a palace flag announcing the queen was in residence."

The pastor's wife eyed the box of donuts. "Do these need to go to the luncheon? Mrs. Henwick should be stopping by, and you can ride over with her."

"Don't get me started on Henwick." Andrea padded across the carpet to the table, plopping herself down and flinging open the box of donuts so hard the fake carboard lid bounced after hitting the table. "It was her idea. We needed 'classics,' she said. She probably wears pearls while she vacuums."

Andrea snatched a beautifully glazed cake donut from the half dozen assorted pastries. "Oh, shoot, I'm so sorry," she mumbled through a mouthful. "I forgot you guys don't eat this stuff. Want me to take them outside? It's cool that you've decided to forsake worldliness and all that."

The sweet scent of fried bread and icing wafted through the dining room.

Twenty years ached in her chest at that scent. The twenty donuts she'd eaten since they had committed to a life of homesteading, simplicity, and service. Twenty years without television, of riding a bike instead of driving a car, of watching him travel the world while she made casseroles for luncheons.

She hated casseroles.

The donuts looked at her, sweet sugary voices whispering that if the pastor's wife *really* wanted to help Andrea be comfortable in the congregation, she should sit and eat one. That's what Jesus would do, wasn't it?

"Is this coffee okay?" Andrea asked as the pastor's wife sat.

The pastor's wife accepted the cup and sipped, catching herself before she groaned with pleasure at the rich, thick brew. "It's fine," she said, then eyed the donuts on the table between them. "And I suppose we don't need to discuss practical applications of Jesus eating with sinners before I indulge in one of these?"

Andrea choked on her donut. "O.M.G. That is the funniest thing anyone has ever said about me. Yeah, Mrs. B. I'll be your sinner."

The pastor's wife looked down at the five donuts looking up at her.

Andrea pushed the box closer. "When I can't decide, I start on the left."

The pastor's wife took the gentle-looking maple bar from the left, admiring the stickiness of the icing and the way the soft rectangle fit so perfectly between her thumb and index finger.

"So anyway," Andrea grabbed a second donut for herself, "I need you to vote with me on the book club picks. The knitting circle will side with Henwick, but I can't read that nonsense." She glared at where *Middlemarch* lay on the floor.

The pastor's wife took her first bite, the soft sweetness melting on her tongue.

"And I also need to know why it's your favorite. It can't be your favorite." Andrea gulped more coffee. "Please tell me the knitting circle is playing a joke on me. Modern women can't idealize this book."

Oh, but she had. Twenty years ago, full of youthful ideals, she'd read *Middlemarch* and considered Dorothea's marriage to Reverend Casaubon inspiring. *That*, she'd thought, was the sort of personal sacrifice that could change the world. If everyday people would find it in themselves to forego immediate satisfaction in order to pursue higher ideals... the possibilities for good would be endless. Love didn't matter nearly so much as making the world a better place.

From down the hall, the washing machine buzzed.

The pastor's wife helped herself to her third and then fourth bite of the sticky, sweet treat melting in her fingers.

"Do you want me to get that?" Andrea asked, nodding towards the laundry room as the machine signaled the end of the cycle again.

"Mm." The pastor's wife filled her mouth with soft fried dough. "It's the Henderson's. Their washer broke."

Andrea snorted. "And Mr. H couldn't fathom a twenty-four-hour period without freshly starched slacks?"

The appliance company couldn't deliver until next week. Mrs. Henderson was surely delighted to not have to do laundry for her high-maintenance husband and five children for a few days.

The oven timer beeped. The rolls needed to be removed.

The pastor's wife licked her fingers, then finished the first half of her donut just as Andrea had—with a long, indulgent gulp of the coffee. This coffee was *good*. Thick and rich, strong. Smelling almost like chocolate, not bitter like the cheap beans the pastor wanted her to buy from bulk bins.

"What does the oven need?" Andrea stood, taking her cup to the kitchen. She stopped halfway across the tattered rug, as if catching herself. Turning from the sink, where the garbage was kept, she peeked into the pantry—the broken door wouldn't open all the way—and grabbed an extra garbage sack. She dropped the coffee cup into the sack and brought it back to the table.

The pastor's wife smiled as she dropped her own cup into Andrea's bag. "Should I be worried how easily you think to hide the evidence?"

"It's a practical life skill, Mrs. B. I'd be grounded for the rest of my life if my parents knew half of what I do."

The pastor's wife raised an eyebrow at the younger woman.

"Oh, come on, it's not like I'm a raging drug addict." Andrea pointed to the hutch displaying the pastor's accomplishments. "I want to be like you two. Help people."

The pastor's wife licked her fingers, shocked to find them empty, the donut finished.

"Here," Andrea pushed the box towards her. "I won't tell if you won't."

"Dare I ask what you're lying to your parents about?"

"I'm supposed to be with my dad on Wednesdays, but that's the only day his girlfriend's off work during the week. Dad thinks I'm in the apartment getting homework done. Mom thinks I'm with Dad… blah, blah. I volunteer down at the rescue mission."

The oven beeped again, reminding the house it needed attention.

"I really am qualified to remove hot things from ovens," Andrea said.

"Shh." The pastor's wife closed her eyes and let her teeth sink into her second donut. "I'm experiencing the divine."

With a laugh, Andrea reached over the table and split the next donut in half, taking the smaller part for herself. "When I'm old and successful, I'll tell young people my pastor's wife influenced me for the better. But secretly I'll know you were just drunk on processed carbs."

"That's flattering. I think."

"You do a lot of good. We should all be trying to be like you."

The pastor's wife almost snorted. This wasn't 'good.' This was a rundown house she couldn't keep up with—had no desire to keep up with—and a makeshift homestead she'd built from reading library books because the pastor didn't want the internet in his home. This was casseroles and chores for other people that they should be doing themselves and ridiculous rules about commercialism that she didn't care about. It was service given begrudgingly because she kept hoping that someday she would do something that really mattered and have people grateful to her for what she'd done.

Not that the volunteer luncheon committee wasn't grateful she'd made twelve casseroles and five dozen rolls and chopped fresh everything needed for four green salads. Not that members of the congregation didn't say thank you when the pastor volunteered her to do their laundry. They did.

She eyed Andrea's copy of *Middlemarch* on the floor.

But when she'd started this twenty years ago, she'd thought it would be a grand and exotic adventure, traveling all over the world, meeting all kinds of people, helping people with basic needs, not just foregoing first-world luxuries. She'd thought she wouldn't be trapped by cultural constraints, like Dorothea's character had been, and that she'd be able to accomplish the kind of work Dorothea hadn't been able to.

The phone rang. A landline, not a cell phone. Even the elderly people in the congregation had cell phones now. She did not.

Andrea eyed the pastor's wife as the phone on the wall finished ringing. "Are you plotting some kind of rebellion against the luncheon today?"

Ignoring the laundry, the oven, the phone. So very uncharacteristic.

And so very predictable. This was exactly what had happened to Dorothea's character—noble sacrifice and aspirations rewarded with disillusionment and disappointment.

Instead of twenty years pursuing ambitious ideals, she'd turned into an empty shell of a person who did nothing but cook and clean and do laundry for people she wasn't entirely sure she cared for.

She wiped her fingers on a napkin, then split the next donut. "They can wait. And no, we're not letting the knitting circle read that trash for the book club."

Andrea grinned. "Can we burn our copies?"

The pastor's wife hesitated.

"I'll bring more donuts," Andrea said. "Next Tuesday. Same time, same place. No one has to know."

"The cream-filled kind?"

"A full dozen."

The phone rang again.

The pastor's wife smiled as she savored the last bites of the donut. "Perfect."

TO RJ WALKER: FROM THE BLOCK ON TOP OF YOUR BRICK

MEG CONDIE

Block who live above Brick say, "No look, Brick."
"Brick not made to look. Brick made to sit still, not move."
- RJ Walker, "Brick"

I've held this wall two decades now.
When I was young gravel, university wasn't an option.
I needed a job, not grand ideals,
So, Block I became, to follow my fathers.

I traveled the world and loved places and cultures…
Saw the value of freedoms you and I both honor.
What I saw as I traveled, being part of this wall and that,
Leads me to think chaos more harmful than borders.

Yes, I said stop, but Brick's youth mistook
Guidance for absolute declaration.
We need clever young bricks to propose ideas,
To challenge the lessons we've learned from our elders.

But Brick has not witnessed the danger chaos permits.
Hotels and smiles are lovely endeavors
Because structure and rules secure our efforts.

I've seen rage and terror Brick's just too young to grasp—
Protected mothers and babes while bombs blasted my back,
Stood in blockades to keep aid workers safe,
Fortified roads to give innocents passage.
Some walls are cruel, and some are to shelter.
Sometimes, like toddlers, we need a divider,
So people can sit and think what to do after.
Yes, ruthless and brutal is the world we all live in.
The tragedy, Brick, is that walls are needed.

I don't have the answers.
My job and purpose were never to think.
I was built to hold lines that keep at least some people safe.
The systems that made me are far from perfection.

The cruelty of my existence is not beyond my awareness;
Fate put me on one side of geographical space,
Now my children have ice cream and great education,
While innocents suffer absolute devastation.
It isn't unnoticed that my place in this wall
Ensures my kids' future while condemning the others'.
I leave that irony to the more philosophically minded.

This, also, young bricks would be wise to consider:
It's not just an idea you smash with your passion,
But built in around me are my father and brother,
Devoting their lives to maintaining this structure.
You want to be pushed and propel innovation,
But if it's my family on which you are broken
We'll each crush the other,
And in the rubble left over

What, exactly, will we have accomplished?

For the young such as you,
Impulse and anger can be quick to overwhelm,
But like any young creature, we must master those passions
If our purpose is change, not just reciprocal agitation.

We have hate to spare,
If Brick hasn't noticed, this wall's confirmation.
Any ol' brick can be violent or cruel.
It takes neither reason nor Magna Cum Laude education.

Push, if you feel that you must.
As I push back, I'll still believe my job is just.
I won't yield my role protecting civilized structure,
Because greater than this, are my decades of terror
That hate will destroy us faster than borders.

THE BREAKOUT

PAT PARTRIDGE

On Wednesday, a big woman in a big hat approached the cash register holding a rust-colored t-shirt with Kokopelli dancing on it.

She smiled as she passed it to me to ring up. "Are you an Indian?"

"No," I said.

Her smile dwindled. "Oh. You look like you might be."

"Looks are deceiving."

"Are you sure?"

I opened my eyes wide and stared, as if in terror. "You're not looking for a scalp, are you?"

"No, no! I, I was just …" She paused. "I hope I didn't offend you."

"That'll be $15.96 including tax. Cash or credit?"

Two minutes later, as she exited the museum, she looked over her shoulder, then turned to her husband.

"He sure looked like an Indian."

That's when I decided to take my first scalp, at least metaphorically.

———

My best friend, Tom Benally, calls me a "half-breed." I call him a "worthless Injun." He is full-blooded Navajo—Diné. I'm not. My father is Navajo, my mom Anglo. They met at college. I speak very little Navajo, a beautiful language. I speak English with a Navajo accent.

I've dealt with identity crap since I was six. An older, wiseass white kid called me a half-breed on the school playground. I didn't know what it meant, but I knew it was an insult.

Some people think it's cool I get to live in both worlds. It's not. Bigotry isn't color blind. Never will be. Nothing comes easier because of my mixed heritage. Maybe it shouldn't. I don't expect it.

Tom and I work at the Northeast Arizona Museum of Native American Heritage. The Anglo visitors outnumber Natives twenty to one. The visitors are curious in a casual way about Native culture. (The "with-it" ones are careful to say "Native American," a term most Natives don't use.) They believe they'll learn something about an exotic culture, one they've seen on TV shows and movies, like visiting a foreign culture without needing a passport.

The Anglos in this area are lauded as "pioneers," not the marauders, conquerors, and land-grabbers they were. At the museum—a repository of history and truth, right?—we downplay the Anglos' brutality. Why? Because—surprise!—the major donors are white. Some burden themselves with white guilt, but the museum doesn't want to rub their faces in their ancestors' perfidies.

Tom was raised on the Navajo reservation, speaks the language, got a degree at Diné College on the reservation. He's also a competitive hoop dancer—came in second at the tribal championships last year.

"Come dance with us," he says. "Learn the Basket Dance, the Sacred Fire Dance. Become your Navajo self."

"Maybe someday," I say. But I don't have a Navajo self. Not sure what that means in my bungled world.

I'm one year away from a master's in archaeology, studying the paltry left-behinds of ancient Pueblo tribes from a thousand years ago. They left no written record, only carvings and paintings on stones, and Anglo scholars have argued over their meaning for going on two hundred years. Now, some Native scholars are joining in the arguments while hundreds of families go without running water or electricity. Yay.

I don't think I'll finish my degree. Too many days it depresses me.

———

It's 3 A.M. on a moonless Saturday night. My colleagues believe I'm camping, not breaking into our museum. My hands shake as I insert the backdoor key I copied. Five seconds inside, I've disabled the alarm. The code is 1864—the year of the Long Walk, the forced relocation of the Navajo from their lands by the U.S. government. Hard to forget.

I wear latex gloves, the kind we use to handle artifacts. I plan to be in and out in ten minutes.

I've decided to break the glass cases holding what I want, even though I know where the keys are. I don't want it to look like an inside job. Insurance will cover a theft.

I move quickly and smash the case holding Anasazi baskets. The one I want is a beautiful basket from the Basketmaker II period. Some pothunters plundering ancestral ruins in the 1960s found it. They got caught. They didn't do any jail time, of course, but the museum got the basket.

I smash the case holding clothing. I take an eye-catching Zuni beaded moccasin likely worn by a child at the end of the 19th century. The beads sparkle in the beam of my flashlight.

I smash the case holding prized pottery. I pass over the stunning red-on-black clay bowl with its perfect zigzag pattern, the museum's prized possession. Instead, I lift out a smaller black-on-white ancestral Puebloan pitcher from around 900 C.E. I've never held it before. It's fragile, having been reconstructed from three separate shards. Archaeologists found it digging in the area where my grandfather's grandfather lived. Vaguely shaped like a bird, it may represent a duck. Hard to tell. I place it gently into a small box padded with paper towels.

I'd never stolen anything more valuable than a pencil, nor imagined I would, but I am feeling exultant. Like I've grasped some pieces of the puzzle that is me.

Tomorrow, I will take the items and repatriate them to their ancestral home. Sort of. I will rebury them at a site excavated long ago where everyone believes anything worthwhile has already been looted. Each item will deteriorate slowly over centuries, as they should.

I glance at my watch. I am behind schedule.

I load the boxes with the basket and the moccasin into my truck quickly. As I exit with the box containing the delicate pitcher, sweat now cascading down my neck, an owl screeches in a nearby tree.

Startled, I drop the box. The sound of the ceramic breaking takes my breath away.

But then I smile. And nod. I leave it behind, knowing the good archaeologists will put it back together. Again.

The basket and moccasin I will still bury, gifts to the past and the unknowable future.

DESICCATED TEARS
MARGOT MONROE

CW: Partner death

"Come walk with me." I held out my hand. She waited a moment, then took it with a ferocity nearing pain. I wrapped my other hand around her forearm, the contrast between my green fingers and her blue skin like a picture of the Earth, land and sea in balance.

… at least it used to be.

The rays of the sinking sun shot silver threads through rosy clouds. A pair of sandhill cranes took flight, wings bigger than their needle-thin bodies. I pulled my hand from her forearm to point them out, following their path across the sky.

Carole laughed, gruff, deep in her throat. "You sighed. I don't know how many sunsets we have watched, and every time you act like it's the first you've ever seen."

A prickle of defensiveness rose in me, but Carole quickly said, "No, I love it."

"I've just never seen *this* sunset before."

She put her hand on my forearm, drawing us closer, hips brushing as we fell into lockstep. "I love it," she repeated. Her shrug transmitted up through my arm. "Millenia of sunsets, and I feel like the only time I've *seen* them is with you. I don't know how—" Her voice faltered, and her fingers dug into my forearm.

The glory of tonight's sunset was from the dust kicked up on Carole's western shore. It was only fitting her eventual end should be heralded with this much beauty and awe and wonder. The truly sublime, bigger than a mortal—or immortal—mind could truly hold or understand.

"You'll watch the sunsets without me." I could only manage a whisper through my parched throat. "The sunsets will remind you of me."

Carole, who I'd never seen cry before, finally broke down. "There is *nothing* that will not remind me of you." She stopped walking and buried her face in her hands, hair like lake foam cascading over her fingers.

I held her shoulders, trying to comfort her and steady myself.

"If I could just *help* you," she managed between sobs, "but any water I'd give you would just…"

Her salty waters would wither my roots faster than the drought could. No naiad should have to watch their lover die of thirst.

I pulled her to me, her head nestled in the space between neck and shoulder.

Her hands, initially clasped over her face, grabbed my tunic, tight fistfuls of linen catching her salty tears.

Carole lived on a timespan of mountain ranges and mammoth calves. A lake, an inland sea lives on a geologic timespan. A weeping willow is the occasional green flash over a sunset in comparison.

I knew my life would flicker briefly, but just like the sunset, I could enjoy it no matter what. With Carole by my side, that had been easy.

The breeze kicked up from the west. I hoped it wouldn't carry too much dust with it, but it probably would. The plants lived in a delicate balance with the salty water, why not add toxic dust to the mix?

The last two hundred years threw the careful dance of equilibrium into chaos. Her waters became more brackish and receded. All the migrating birds, like those sandhill cranes, would be left without food, without a home…

The same way Carole's heart would be left without a home and sustenance.

"Jane, I can't do this. I *know* this isn't right. I won't let them… I won't let you just…" She drew a deep breath, then looked up into my face. "I won't let you die without them knowing it."

My throat tightened again, making my parched mouth drier. "I was always going to die."

She looked away, mouth pursing. "Not like this. Not in your prime. Not of… not of thirst." She looked up into the sky, rosy twilight giving way to night. "Not when there is enough rain, but it gets siphoned off when the rest of the world is dying." Tears of rage spilled down her cheeks.

"I'm sorry." I wiped her cheek, the deep ache of thirst calling for that moisture pinched between thumb and index finger.

"Don't be sorry." More salty tears flowed down her cheeks. "You have nothing to be sorry for."

I shook my head. "I knew what would happen to me and that you'd end up alone. And still, I pursued you."

"I could *never* regret you, Jane. All those years and sunsets. They never meant anything until you. I did what I needed to; I kept my lake, I managed the animals, and now…" She drew a deep breath, then wiped her face and held out her hand to me. "Let's walk."

We settled in together, holding hands until she tucked her arm around my waist, our hips bumping.

I sighed, settling my head on her shoulder. The world has shown me such wonders. I've been loved, I've loved, my heart is full with the sights of the world.

Her cheekbone pressed into the top of my head, and I breathed in the moment of calm and caring and support. *This* is what the world should be. Mutual support and respect and care. And the resources to offer those things.

The chorus of bugs rose like the hum of a bird's feast. Quieter than it used to be, with fewer bugs than there used to be, birds as well. Just a gradual decline of all things. My decline faster than most.

Carole's hand tightened on my hip, the bone obvious beneath the skin.

"I don't want to stay here." Her *without you* hung in the air.

I put my hand over Carole's, holding her close and giving her all the comfort I could. Trapped here, as her own shoreline shrinks, watching her approaching demise.

"I want to raze it all." She gritted her teeth, then pressed into me tighter.

I was just a single tree, finite in so many ways, but Carole reached deep into the paths of time. A world where alfalfa was grown at the cost of all this wonder. Well, maybe the world deserved it.

"You're not going to tell me to be gentle?" Carole finally said.

I shook my head against her shoulder. "If it was just me, then I would. But you are…" I choked on words like ashes in my throat. "You should exist beyond time. Beyond the kind of time of living things. Leaves and branches fall in a lakebed, and that's the *only* way they achieve any sort of immortality… preserved through you. The only way *I* reach immortality is through this." I set my hand over her heart, that precious place she kept so hidden.

"I don't know how I can live without you now." Carole drew a deep breath and looked to the deep, dark, east sky. Stars sparkled over the Wasatch mountains. "I don't know how long before I am nothing but a muddy marsh, but if I have to go, they do as well."

"Is there *anything* we can do?" I whispered. A shifting fault, an asteroid, a shudder through the bones of the universe, an actual reason for her demise is one thing. The siphoning of water from the natural world is a travesty.

"If there was, we would have done it when the first leaf on

your tree thought about turning yellow."

I wrapped both arms around her, one clinging to her shoulder, forearm pressed against her heart, the other around her waist.

"So, how will you raze the world?" It sounded like a droll question at a dinner party.

A chuckle emanated from her chest. "What little water I have, I will give to the clouds, so they loose it on the mountains in deep drifts of snow. I'd guess the temperature will be as inconstant as everything else. It'll get warm, then hot. Imagine all the flooding."

"That will keep you going for longer." The idea of extending Carole's life appealed to me, even though I guessed her life's only goal would be to wreak havoc on all the people who had done this to us.

Her arm tightened around me, but she made a noncommittal noise.

The marshy shore sucked at my steps; the soft, fetid mud exposed for the first time in years. I stumbled, not strong enough to pull my foot from the sticky mud.

Carole grabbed me, absorbing my momentum. I knew what a pebble felt like, dropped in a pond. Tiny ripples that settle into nothing.

"You're so light."

Carole steadied me, then herded me up the shore to firmer sand.

"I don't think I have much time left." We both knew it, but we had never said it like that.

"I know."

"So, what's next, after the flooding?"

We started walking again, toward the home we shared. A lovely cottage midway between my tree and her shore.

"I wish the clouds could take the water away from my watershed." She sighed, a hint of the fury her dust storms could carry washed over my arm. "But that's a long distance. Once my water level drops, I'll let that dust fly. Arsenic will fill the air. Imagine a blizzard, but with a dust so fine it settles in your lungs. Filled with

minerals that wreck livers and hurt the children, so many things."
A pause, then a guilt gilded moan rose from her chest. "I don't
want to hurt children."

I gave her a squeeze, holding her as tight as I could.

"*You're* not hurting children." I shifted my hand from her
shoulder to her heart. "Instead, *they* are letting it happen. How
long have we watched this slow retreat of your waters? We've
been *seeing* this happen. When was the last time buffalo calves
frisked on your shores? Love, *none* of this is your fault. What
happens to them, regardless of whether we want it, well, that is
on them. We are victims in this, just as their children will be."

"I don't actually *want* to raze it all to the ground. I am just so
angry…"

"I know." She leaned her head against my shoulder, and I
kissed her temple softly, like absolution. "I know."

"They don't know we're dangerous."

I nodded, kissing her temple once again.

She stopped, then said, "Gods, look at that sunset." The last
light faded as the western stars twinkled into view. The
extraordinary beauty of the sunset was another reminder of the
end. The cycle of the sun was broken for me. I wouldn't see it rise,
just like the cycle of Carole's waters evaporating in the blinding
heat of summer and replenishing with the melting of the snow.
What cycle would break next?

"Do you think they know?" Carole asked.

"That they're on the brink of catastrophe?"

She nodded.

"I don't know," I said. "If they did, you think they'd do something. The signs are all there."

"All this time, trying to control nature, and they don't know
that they're part of it. And when they try to be clever, they can't
see anything beyond the immediate consequences. And they only
care about the consequences that benefit them. Any negative
consequences are someone else's problem" She snorted. "I wish
they knew that they're still part of nature."

Our home was just in sight, my tree in the distance, tucked up on a hillock, yellow leaves littering the ground and bench beneath it.

"Can we sit?"

"Of course."

It's funny, the little things you don't think you'd miss. The slick prickle of sweat on the forehead, or the clammy sensation of holding hands with someone for too long. Being a creature out in the world with your fellow creature. I didn't think I'd miss it, but I knew it meant the imminent end.

She settled me on the bench, the falling leaves just loud enough to be heard over the chorus of bugs. She sat next to me, arm still warm across my back, hand clamped to my hip.

"Are you comfortable?"

"I have everything I could want in this moment." The next moments though? The ones with Carole wracked by grief, anger, and loneliness? The ones where Carole would let that anger and grief out on an unsuspecting but culpable world? Those moments terrified me. Instead, I sank into this sensation of Carole, warm and buoyed up the same way that her saline waters carried me.

"I love you."

I relaxed, leaning into her more heavily. In a world of so many wonders, funny that three words could be the most moving of them all.

"I'll always be with you. Always right here." I tucked my hand against her heart, feeling those beats while it breaks.

She nodded once, pulling me tighter to her chest.

One single, salty tear hit my cheek. She still gave me all the water she had. The final leaf fell from my tree with a sigh and a whisper.

I didn't know what kind of danger the world faced now, but it was all preventable.

I tightened my grasp of the tunic under my fingers, and like the final leaf on the tree, slipped away on another sigh and a whisper.

SCRAPPERS OF THE GREAT STARSHIP

JOHN M. OLSEN

The scrappers who scavenged for treasures in the ancient crash site of the Great Starship were so far down the food chain that favors and good luck were a distant dream. Overlapping craters marked the landscape with hints of treasures that had fallen from the sky, if only you had enough drive and luck. But mostly, the craters were a prison with no walls. Escape required finding something so valuable it would propel you from squalor and stench to a life of ease far away from the craters. Shayden had seen such luck strike exactly zero times in his eighteen years.

Pickings were light and growing lighter by the day. Shayden and his digging partner would have to move soon. "Hey, Vannic, does your uncle still have the saw that cuts through metal plating?" A sheet of rust-free metal protruded from the dusty ground, begging to be harvested if he could just detach it from the remaining skeletal structure embedded in the ground.

His friend and digging partner laughed. "He said it broke. I think a scrap buyer had someone steal it from him, and he's too scared to confront them."

Lack of a saw meant no large pieces of scrap metal. "We should head to another crater tomorrow, but for today, we do this the hard way. Can we lever this out?" Shayden picked up Vannic's walking stick and prodded the ground. If he could bend the sheet, then metal fatigue would eventually cause a break and leave him with a prize good enough to earn his dinner from one of the local scrap buyers who worked with independent scrappers like him.

"Give me that walking stick before you break it. Do you know how hard it was to find that one?" Not only was Vannic his best and only friend, he was clever, and he could scrounge and reuse stuff like nobody else.

After taking over with the stick, Vannic finally worked out a spot where he could place it for the right leverage. "There. Now lean into it."

Salty sweat beaded on Shayden's face from the physical stress and the heat of the sun. Eventually, the sheet squealed and bent far enough to crease the metal.

Vannic waved his hands and put a finger to his lips, then pointed toward a trail winding through nearby stacks of stone rubble and packed dirt.

With a nod, Shayden eased behind the sheet he'd just bent, and Vannic picked up a rock and threw it in a shallow arc, hitting a distant pillar of rock where it bounced noisily down the far side. Then he dropped and rolled into the shadows under a rock with an overhang. The silence stretched.

Soon, footfalls reached Shayden's straining ears. At least three people approached. Vannic had always had better hearing, and it had saved them in the past.

"You heard the noise, same as I did. Someone that can make metal bend could be useful to the boss. She needs more workers." It had to be Bart and his lackeys, but Shayden didn't dare peek around the steel plate to make sure.

One of Bart's helpers said, "She wouldn't need so many if they stopped dying. Nothing here. I heard something past the twin pillars over there as we walked up." He waved toward where Vannic had thrown a rock.

The three toughs moved on, and Vannic rolled out from under

his rock overhang. "They're gone now. Quiet, or they might come back."

Glancing between Vannic and the metal, Shayden said, "I bet we can damp the sound if we wrap your shirt around it."

With everything cobbled together and properly wrapped, Shayden and Vannic bent the metal back and forth until it gave way with a muffled clank. The sheet was big enough for a smith to turn into a sizeable plate or a tray, and the trade fee would feed them both that night.

Vannic put his shirt back on. "If we come back tomorrow, we can dig out and break off another piece that size, but the leverage will be tricky. I'll need a bigger stick." That was the trouble with a lot of the scrap. It came in such enormous pieces, it couldn't be claimed without tools beyond the reach of scrappers.

Dusk fell, calling an end to the workday. As Shayden led the way between the twin pillars, three figures materialized from the shadows.

One of Bart's lackeys said, "I told you they were back there."

Bart held out a metal bar longer than his arm to block the way as his bodyguards produced knives. "You won't be needing that metal sheet, Shayden."

The lackey reached out and took the hard-won scrap.

"That was for our dinner. What are we supposed to do now?" It wasn't fair, but Shayden didn't put much stock in life being fair.

"I've got a job for you. My boss is putting a team together to look for something in the big crater."

"That death trap? You've got to be kidding me." Shayden's father wasn't the only one to enter the largest crater of the crash site and never come out. He was as likely to find a skeleton as salvage.

Bart gave a sly smile as he cradled his improvised weapon. "I'll get you some food to make up for your stupid sheet of steel. The food's waiting at the big crater camp. Turns out that hard work makes people hungry."

This was exactly why Shayden had spent so much time and

effort dodging Bart and his ilk who worked for the less reputable scrap buyers. Some were little more than slave traders, driving scrapper teams into the ground, then replacing them like a faulty tool when they broke.

If he and Vannic ran, they might get away, or they might get beaten or killed. If he went along, it wouldn't even help to drag his feet. It would only mean a longer wait before Shayden could eat. His stomach grumbled from the long day of work, betraying his hunger.

He gave Bart his best glare. "Fine. We'll go." He and Vannic could run away later and find a new scrap buyer on the long tail of the crash site, as far as possible from here.

The hike to the crater lasted an hour, most of it in the dark over trails he'd never memorized. It seemed that Bart had an excellent memory, since they rounded a small crater lip to find a camp complete with a cooking pot over a fire.

The scent of a spicy stew wafted over the small camp. Shayden's stomach grumbled again as Vannic stumbled along behind with his walking stick.

Bart prodded them both from behind. "Over there to the tent."

With one last glance at the stewpot, Shayden headed to the tent where one of the lackeys held the flap open.

Upon entering, the smell was the first thing to hit Shayden: A hint of the stew from the firepit, but with a touch of fragrance, like the flowers he'd seen the previous summer out past the craters where hunters and ranchers worked. His father had taken him there to trade.

It seemed like they had a better life out there, but his father had drilled it into him that none were to be trusted, and that everyone worked under some sort of taskmaster in the end.

Rugs covered the floor, and a table sat in the middle of the tent. A narrow cot sat behind the table against the tent wall. A woman in her thirties sat at the table, watching their approach.

Bart followed Shayden and Vannic in. "Here are the ones I told you about. This one is Shayden. The other, I think, is

Vannic. They broke this free." He set the metal plate on her desk.

"Manners, Bart. You didn't introduce me. I'm Morgane, and this is my camp."

Shayden nodded to her in acknowledgment. "I'd say it's nice to meet you, but …" He gestured toward Bart.

She smiled, but more like a predator than a friend. "Yes. Well, I pay him to follow instructions. But you, on the other hand, were scroungers with no master. Rudderless, getting by day to day. I'm here to change all that. I'll start by giving you regular meals. In exchange for keeping you fed and healthy, you'll work for me in the big crater."

It wouldn't do any good to argue with her, so Shayden chose to humor her instead. "And what are your scroungers searching for?"

She reached beneath her table and produced a shoulder-mounted weapon, laying it on the table before her. "Power. A team found this gun months ago, and now I need the power modules to go with it. Without those power modules, it's nothing but a fragile club."

There was more than one kind of power, and Morgane had plenty of power over others. Now she was using her psychological power to gain more tangible leverage.

"Do you know where to look?" If he sounded interested, they might survive long enough to flee.

"I know where this came from." She patted the weapon. "You'll dig there tomorrow. Until then, we make sure you stick around. Bart, get some shackles."

Vannic spoke after being silent for the whole meeting. "We were promised food. If we starve, we can't dig."

"Fine. Chain them to the cooking area." Turning to Shayden and Vannic, she continued. "You can eat whatever you can scrape out of the cooking pot when you clean it. Everybody eats, but nobody eats for free."

There was less than a single portion left, and what remained had crisped around the edges. Shayden didn't complain as he and Vannic split the meager meal.

Bart tossed a couple of blankets at them. "I'll take you to the dig site in the morning."

A night curled up on the dirt wrapped in a blanket was nothing like the hammock he was used to. The night was darker than most, with the Three Sisters having set early into the night. Some said they were tiny moons. Others made fantastic claims of them being the source of the Great Starship that crashed. Either way, he didn't sleep well, and he woke with a sore back when Bart dropped a small loaf of bread on each of their blankets.

"Get up." Bart prodded Shayden with his foot. "Eat your bread while we march."

Soon, Shayden and Vannic were chained in a line with other scrappers, prodded forward on a trail that rose to the edge of the big crater, then traced a zig-zag path down the inside. As forced marches go, it was barely long enough to eat his bread.

Shayden gazed across metal wreckage and stone outcroppings in the base of the largest of the craters and crouched to rest for a moment. The dry bread had made him thirsty.

Vannic tapped his walking stick against a metal cylinder protruding from the debris. The vibration made its way back up through Shayden's feet as dust filtered down from the tops of twisted metal spires. The other scrappers glared as they covered their heads and glanced around at the swaying debris. This was why most scrappers stayed away.

The one at the head of the line turned to Bart and said, "I don't want to dig with the new guys. They'll get us all killed."

The other scrappers murmured their agreement.

Vannic glanced around, then said, "You can lock us to that pillar and leave us here to dig." He pointed to what might have once been an anchor ring.

"Fine," said Bart. "If you don't find anything here, you don't eat."

He unlocked the two from the line of scrappers, then looped a long wire rope through as Vannic held his arms out as wide as the shackles allowed, then gave Shayden a look until he did the same. Bart locked both ends of the wire rope to the anchor ring protruding from a twisted metal panel.

Bart turned to his thugs. "Let's take the rest to the main dig. These two will scrounge here today."

Shayden held his hands out. "No water?"

"Dig for it." Bart and his crew laughed as they led the rest of the scrappers away.

Once the others had marched a stone's throw away, Vannic said, "I thought they'd never leave us alone." He forced a loop of the cable through the shackle on his left wrist, looped it over his hand, and was free from the cable.

"How did you do that?"

Vannic peered off into the distance toward the other scrappers. "Well, first, I spotted this metal cylinder that would conduct a nice hit into the ground."

"No. The cable. How did you get it off?"

Leaning close, Vannic tucked the cable through the shackle at Shayden's wrist, looped it over his hand, then pulled it back through the shackle. He was loose. "They hooked us up the same way last night, just looping the cable through our arms instead of lacing it through the shackle."

"And you never told me we could get free?" His friend might be clever, but he wasn't a great communicator.

"They would have just chased us down. Too many guards. I spotted five along the rim as we came in, and that means the only way past is within the crater itself. There's too much tall junk here to see us, but they would notice if we made a break for it over the rim."

Shayden examined the precarious boulders and jutting metal scraps. "That scrapper was right about the danger. One wrong move and we'll never make it out. But if we find the power module Morgane is after, we're home free."

"If she doesn't kill us or keep us locked up forever. Why

would she ruin a good thing?"

Shaden let out a snorting laugh. "Why do you always do that? I had a perfectly pleasant image in my head, and you killed it with your talk of eternal slavery and doom."

The area had seen a little foot traffic recently from Morgane's scrappers, but otherwise, it was untouched. No signs of digging, cutting, or moving of anything. Such an area bore enough metal to support several scrappers, but he wasn't after metal to trade. If he found what Morgane wanted, at least he could negotiate. And now, he wasn't being watched. "Ideas? I say we start moving metal sheeting. Even if Morgane is after something specific, she needs to fund this hunt somehow. Let's get started."

By midday, they had a stack of sheet steel that would normally pay for a week of supplies. Shayden reached for the next piece, and his foot dropped into an open space as a large platform tilted. Quick reflexes kicked in, and he grabbed an edge. If the platform tipped any more, he would slide into the dark hole near his feet.

"Don't move," came Vannic's panicky but intense voice. "I think I can brace it so we don't fall to our deaths." Vannic held to the top of the sloped metal platform with one hand and his walking stick with the other.

A quick look down the new slope showed a dark opening that continued down for dozens of meters. Maybe more with how dark it was. "I'm as still as a mouse. Tell me when I can breathe again."

A few tense moments later, Vannic pulled the high end of the platform down so it sat level once more. Somewhere behind Shayden, he grumbled and cursed, then finally walked around and stood in front of Shayden on the plate that had shifted. "You're good to move now. This whole plate is balanced on a fulcrum, but it will stay while my brace is there."

Turning, Shayden saw the walking stick jammed in end-to-end to prevent the pivoting sheet from moving. Peering below, he saw a set of handholds descending into the dark, and grinned. Shaden had always dreamed of exploring an intact section of the Great

Starship. This wasn't the way he'd envisioned it, but the thrill drew him.

"Let's go. There's got to be something down there."

Vannic gazed into the darkness below, then tested the first handhold. "Seems stable for now."

Shayden followed him down dozens of handholds, finally finding a tilted floor far below. Dim illumination reached them from the opening. The deepest edge of the floor was littered with bones, some human, and some from small creatures.

A smell of old rot and dust filled the air. Bent and twisted metal walls showed tunnels running off in two directions, but the light dropped off to nothing a short distance from the wide shaft they'd climbed down.

Vannic kicked the bones a couple of times. "I see nothing useful. These are either decades old, or something down here eats everything down to the bones."

"Such a cheery thought. Now I get to worry about being ambushed and eaten. Let's see how far the light reaches. I don't want to hit another weak piece of floor and drop even deeper."

Vannic laughed nervously. "So, now you're full of cheery thoughts, too."

One path led slightly down, so Shayden chose that one, then felt his way along as it became harder and harder to see. The faint smell of bones and rot faded with the light. Despite the buckled metal, the walls had been solid the whole way with no doors or side passages, but a gradual turn cut off the light. Not even the noise of the surface wind penetrated this deep.

"Nothing this direction. Want to try the other way?"

Vannic stood between Shayden and the tunnel they'd traversed, showing a dim silhouette. "We've got no branches or side passages yet. We can go by feel for a bit without risk of getting lost."

Shayden crept forward on his hands and knees along one wall while Vannic covered the other, both feeling their way to make sure the floor didn't drop away. Working his way around small holes in the floor slowed him to a crawl, but he discovered they were all on his side of the hall. None of the holes were big enough to enter, but any one of them could break an ankle.

The floor was bare, but it took a lot of time to search with tired fingers. "It's no use. We need candles. I hate to say it, but we may need Bart's help."

Vannic said, "Like he'd let us live after finding anything promising. Finding this tunnel might be enough to get us killed."

It was a fair point. Shayden stood and threw his hands in the air in frustration, nearly breaking his knuckles on the shadowed ceiling. It hadn't been this low where they entered.

"Let's check the ceiling on our way back." Shayden ran his fingers along the ceiling, retracing the path he'd crawled, avoiding the holes. They needed to get out before Bart and his lackeys returned for them, and he had no way to tell time underground.

Before he was back to where he could see the dim light of the entrance, he rapped his knuckles on a protrusion hanging down from the ceiling, and he let out a muffled curse. Tracing around the edge, it had a rectangular shape with sharp corners. The bottom face had a handhold, but if there was a latch, he couldn't tell. "I found a box on the ceiling. We must be walking on a wall."

"What kind of box?"

"I don't know. It's boxy and has a handle."

Vannic bumped into Shayden, then ran his hands over the box. "I don't recognize this sort of handle, but if I were a handle designer, I'd make it easy to open. If this wall over here is the floor …"

Vannic fumbled past, then rotated to face the box from another direction. "… I'd make it swing out this way."

He tugged, releasing a latch. Several objects tumbled out, striking Shayden on the head and shoulders on their way to the floor. "Ow. Are you trying to knock my brains out?"

"Oops, sorry. At least I got it open, right?"

Shayden dropped back to his knees and felt around until he

set his hands on a block the size of two fists. "I've got one."

"Me too," said Vannic. "These are heavy, whatever they are."

The shape and size didn't seem to match the weapon Morgane had shown him, but there was no way to be sure in the dark. "Whatever they are, we should probably take them and disappear instead of turning them over. This is old tech, and it might still work."

Vannic said, "Maybe we can dodge those rim guards by skirting to the side first."

It was a terrible plan, but it was better than giving Morgane something that might let her take over and dominate all the scrap buyers, or maybe even kill off her competition. "Maybe we should leave them down here in case they're really battery packs."

Vannic laughed. "I thought you wanted to buy your way into a life of ease. I don't know how much these boxes are worth, but old tech might get you what you want."

Shayden weighed the risks and the reward, and he came up with the same solution. "Let's do it. We can come back for more later."

Climbing with one hand full took a lot longer as he held the heavy block to his chest, but soon he reached a hand up to the surface, only to have someone grab him and haul him the rest of the way out of the covered shaft.

"Looks like we found our runaway, boys!" Bart and one of his thugs stood to either side of the hole at the edge of the large metal plate. "And it looks like Shayden found something for us."

Shayden would have held onto the odd box, but getting stabbed seemed like a bad idea. He handed it over, working frantically for some plan that might still help Vannic escape. "I'd never run away, but Vannic is long gone. He took off deeper into the crater after you left."

Bart examined the box. "It's too big, but it's a power module of some kind. I think it's just too bad that Shayden has to die in a tragic accident."

"I bet we can find more of those modules in that little hole," said the scrapper who had not wanted to work with Shayden. "Enough to make us all rich. I'll kill Shayden myself to get a bigger share."

Shayden backed up, drawing their eyes away from the hole as Vannic eased his way up to crouch behind the threatening team. Vannic could run while Shayden looked for a way to not be murdered.

Vannic locked eyes for a moment with Shayden. He waved his hands, motioning for Shayden to back up. He took a couple of casual steps away from the pit, hoping to draw his captors with him. "Look, we can talk about this, can't we?"

Weapons came out, and the other scrappers cheered Bart on.

Behind Vannic, Bart's other thug jumped out from behind a large metal pipe. "Got ya." He reached for Vannic, but he missed as they both lurched toward the group of scrappers.

Shayden had already done the math, and he didn't see a way to survive. All he could do is watch as the second thug swung a knife at Vannic.

A deft twist kept Vannic away from the blade, but Shayden could only watch as his friend whipped his arm back and threw his power module. He missed everyone, but then, in a horrifying flash of insight, Shayden understood. He leaped backwards off the large metal plate just as the power module hit the walking stick, knocking it loose.

Vannic launched himself into the air as the plate tipped. One of the scrappers tried to jump after him, but they were still hooked together into a labor gang.

Everyone standing on the plate screamed and scrambled, but it was too late. They dropped into the pit as the plate tilted, then snapped loose and dropped into the hole after them with a great crash.

Shayden stood alone on the surface.

He crept over to the edge and took in the scene. Part way down, the plate had wedged itself flat, covering the path down. An arm poked out from one edge, the only sign of the loss of life.

The others would contribute to the piles of bones at the bottom of the drop.

Then he looked back up to the far side to see Vannic hanging from a protruding pipe by both hands. "A little help would be nice."

Moments later, he hefted his friend up.

Shayden shook his head at the waste of it all. Still, it would be a pity to come out of it empty-handed. "I thought we were going to die there for a bit. Grab your power brick. It's time to go."

Vannic stood and looked toward the far edge of the pit, then up toward the crater rim. "Mine fell in, just like yours did. Unless you have a winch or a cutting torch, we've got nothing."

They might as well try jumping to the Three Sisters as hope for the right equipment to reach the fabulous wealth promised below. Nobody had what it would take to get that plate dislodged, and there was no such thing as good luck.

Then again, they were alive, and there was another thing going in their favor. Shayden slapped the edge of the pit. "Morgane will assume we're down there with the rest of them. Let's get out of here before the rim guards investigate."

Sticking to the marked paths was safer, but they would be easy to find if they went that way. Reluctantly, Shayden led them off the trail and parallel to the rim through uncharted dangers.

Hours later, after picking their way through a twisted metal forest, they stood on the rim far away from where Vannic had seen Morgane's guards.

Shayden sat, exhausted and parched. Vannic collapsed beside him in no better condition. It had grown dark as they climbed. Shayden clapped his friend on the shoulder, kicking up a small cloud of dust. "We can start over at one of the smaller craters. We wanted to move on to a better spot anyway, right?"

The chirps of tiny night creatures sounded as they found a well-worn path lit by the faint light of the Three Sisters. "Fine. We'll start over just like you said, but you owe me a new walking stick."

THE PLATINUM OPTION
C.W. ALLEN

Malcolm Turlington smoothed his mustache in the reflection of his com link screen and checked his teeth for errant specks of sushi.

BZZZZT. The ghostly green holo-projection of his assistant's face flickered to life in the air above the desk. "Your one o'clock appointment is here early, Mr. Turlington. Should I ask Mrs. Barrister-Scoville to wait?"

Malcolm smirked. Early, eh? The freeze-dried foods heiress was known for being fashionably late in most social circles. She must be nervous. *Excellent.*

"No, Jonathan, show her in." He stood as the carved mahogany door slid open, disappearing into the wall beside it. "Ah, Mrs. Barrister-Scoville! So good to meet you in person at last! Please, have a seat." He gestured benevolently at the penguin-pelt upholstered chair in front of the desk.

"Oh—Sophie, Mr. Turlington! Call me Sophie. No need for formality among equals." She set her purse on the desk (designer, of course, Malcolm noted, but from last season's line), smoothed the front of her brushed wool skirt suit, and lowered herself gracefully into the chair. "Thank you for working me in on such short notice," she cooed. "Of course, we should have squared this away years ago, but what with managing a busy company, things do tend to get away from you."

Throwing lavish parties, keeping her degenerate son's antics out of the news, tending to a flock of vicious guard peacocks... Malcolm didn't really care how the heiress frittered away her time, but managing her late father's company certainly wasn't on the list—she had "people" for that. Her timing in securing one of Ancestry Data Conglomerate's coveted concierge appointments was no coincidence. No doubt about it, Mrs. Barrister-Scoville had a *problem*. And when the rich had problems, money tended to start migrating. He just needed to herd it in the right direction.

He slapped on his greasiest smile and eased into the pitch. "As your Legacy Concierge, I am honored to help you navigate the data management avenues Ancestry Data Conglomerate has available. Avenues *not* available on the general consumer kiosks, of course. Our typical customers are mostly interested in finding a specific record from an ancestor or two—the deed to Grandma's beach cottage, or whether their third great grandfather preferred sweet pickles or spicy ones. Boring, sentimental, commonplace things. And of course, it's simple enough to make such information available to the masses. But we recognize that our clients of a higher caliber are anything but typical. They require a more... *comprehensive* vision."

Sophie batted her spidery false eyelashes at him. "*Exactly*, Mr. Turlington. Comprehensive. I knew you'd understand."

"Is the Speedy Eats company interested in creating a brand origin museum, then? We could certainly provide you with all the necessary data from your late father and grandfather. Early product design sheets, vintage advertising, holographic scans of the founders at different ages—"

She waved a manicured hand impatiently, swatting the notion away like an irritating insect. "Fine, fine. I'll have the publicity department contact someone about all that. The past is all well and good, but I prefer to look to the future. Or the future's past, I suppose. Laying the groundwork for future legacies, if you catch my meaning."

Ah. This wasn't about the company at all. Or her ancestors. She wanted to lock down her *personal* data. Fascinating…

Malcolm painted on an expression of polite puzzlement, silently inviting the woman to continue spilling secrets.

Sophie took a moment to pat her fashionable blue-with-gold-leaf hairdo into place before elaborating. "Taking the helm of an influential family is such a profound responsibility, and I take that duty seriously. My father and grandfather didn't pull themselves out of the dust of humanity for their own benefit—obviously, they did it to improve the world for their descendants, and I want to secure that legacy for my family as well. Build the castle on a solid foundation, you know? And that foundation will be far more stable if we don't hand marauders ammunition to undermine it with. I need to make sure the data my family generates *today* can't be put to improper use in the future."

"Naturally!" Malcolm agreed, as if he too was burdened with polishing the public image of generations of self-centered industrialists. "Ancestry Data Conglomerate has just the remedy for this dilemma: the Platinum Option.

"Lots of people want to limit the data generated by their everyday choices. Paranoid consumers who can't bear the thought of their purchasing and entertainment habits being scrutinized, or common criminals evading a digital trail. But keeping their data off the beaten path has its drawbacks. Every interaction with modern society leaves digital litter behind. Everything they buy or watch or read, someone behind the scenes wants to scour for trends. Every time they look up travel directions, or even just travel with a com link in their pocket, blinking neon arrows point to betray their whereabouts, metaphorically speaking. To avoid it all, they'd have to go off the grid. Which these days, pretty much means being a cave hermit. Not a very swanky place to host parties, I'm afraid."

At the words "cave hermit," Sophie grimaced like Malcolm had suggested something unthinkably disgusting, like serving bologna sandwiches at a cocktail party. Or any of the food her company produced, for that matter. "Surely, you can't expect me to do that!" she protested. "I have a company to run. An image to protect. A legacy to secure. I can't do all that if I'm afraid to use anything with a screen!"

Malcolm nodded solemnly, trying to swallow his glee. She was taking the bait like a greedy goldfish. Now, to set the hook.

"Of course," he soothed. "Those are burdens *regular* people just can't understand. They want all the answers to their petty problems to be at their fingertips. The salve for their worries should be instant, and preferably free. They don't see the bigger picture, as you and I do. If the service is free, then they're not the customer—they're the *product*. Their data is ours to use as we see fit or sell to others to use. Squeezing profit from the oblivious public's information is ADC's bread and butter, and usually the public finds that a fair trade. But you and I understand: you get what you pay for."

Malcolm leaned meaningfully into the last few words, giving each just a touch of extra weight. Concierge data management was never cheap, but the actual rates were... well, the preferred industry term was "proprietary." Which is just business-speak for "secret, and never the same twice." He was free to push this contract to the breaking point. He could almost taste the commission a legacy contract of this caliber would cook up.

"With the protection offered by the Platinum Option," he continued, "you can rest easy knowing your data will be safe from prying eyes. All historic data from the entire Barrister-Scoville genetic line will be placed on a blackout block, and new data generated from the immediate family members you designate will be carefully archived on a private server. You may access your protected data at any time by providing a genetic sample and your key code to a data banker at any of our offices all over the world. Off-world offices have a slightly longer response time to call up the requested information, I'm afraid, but are also available if you have a need while vacationing on Luna, Mars, or an orbital resort."

At this, Sophie's eyebrows creased together. At least, they would have if years of cosmetic injections had allowed such a vulgar thing as a crease to form. But they definitely twitched.

"Private server?" she asked. "I really just wanted the data deleted. Or preferably never collected in the first place."

"I'm afraid that's impossible," Malcom lied through his bleached teeth. "ADC controls the storage and analysis of consumer data, not the access points that generate it. And there are international compliance laws, mandatory sequestering periods and such. I'm sure you understand." He genuinely hoped she did *not* understand how little regulation his industry had, but he put on his practiced Resigned Perseverance face all the same. Treating curious customers like they were already in the know was a tried and true strategy for squashing questions—they were always too embarrassed to admit they didn't have a clue what he was talking about, so they played along admirably. The Emperor's Tailor ploy had never failed him yet.

Malcolm flipped over one of his business cards and scribbled the biggest number he could think of on the back. Then he tacked one more zero on the end for good measure. He slid the card across the desk and watched Sophie's face with barely constrained amusement as she read the price of her salvation.

She blinked. But only once. Perhaps he should have been a bit more ambitious…

"I don't know," Sophie wavered. "It's just fancy access suites, after all. Champagne and caviar while I wait for a banker to hand over information that's already mine. The general public can't access a living person's data in the first place. And even for historic data, they'd need to prove they're a direct relative. Putting all my information in a pretty box doesn't seem worth this kind of investment…"

Malcolm wasn't fooled. She was just haggling over price at this point. Time to drive the point home.

"Don't think of our private servers and luxury access banks as mere wrapping paper," he insisted. "They're not flimsy decorations. Think of them as vaults. Safes. Guardians. After all," he added casually, "your data is still out there whether you choose to manage it or not. It would be a shame if someone with selfish, malicious designs were to get hold of it. All perfectly legal, you understand. It's not just hackers we're protecting you from. It's our other customers."

Sophie's eyes went wide, and she sucked in a ragged breath. She couldn't look more shocked if he had pulled a gun on her. Malcolm's paternal smile held firm. She was trapped, and now they *both* knew it. She hadn't been on ADC's radar before—just one more faceless consumer among billions. But now that they knew she had something worth hiding, they'd auction her data off to the highest bidder.

"I see," she said, her voice quavering. There was a brief pause before she continued. "What form of payment do you prefer? Check? Wire transfer? Stock options?"

For a wild moment, he was tempted to ask for payment in blood, just to see how she'd react. Actually—they *would* be needing some of her blood. But just enough for a genetic sample. "Wire transfer will be fine," he said at last. "My assistant will provide you with the encrypted routing code on your way out."

Sophie nodded weakly and tottered to her feet, her spindly high heels stabbing deep into the plush carpeting, and showed herself out of the office. She was too distracted to offer a handshake to conclude their business, but Malcolm didn't mind. Handshakes were free. Disposable. Meaningless. Anything with real value was *taken*, not offered.

Malcolm allowed himself a moment to savor his victory. But only a moment. There was work to be done. He swiped open the analysis algorithm and adjusted the parameters. In less than a heartbeat, it coaxed a conclusion from his newest customer's data. *Gotcha.*

He scrolled down the lines of cached decisions. Which celebri-

ties' parties she'd been invited to, her political campaign contribu-
tions, her entire family's voting records, the locations of various
tax shelters she was squirreling her money away in. Where her
family vacationed, what entertainment they watched, every
product they purchased and business they set foot in. The names
of every lawyer, trick accountant, and public relations guru on her
payroll (and how much they were paid). The legal status of her
household servants (and how little they were paid). With all that
data shielded from public view, Sophie Barrister-Scoville could
pretend to be whoever she wanted. Or whoever she thought the
public wanted. Her shiny new contract kept the raw information a
secret, of course, but not the conclusions ADC's software might
draw from it.

He buzzed his assistant's com link. "Jonathan, put in a call to
Senator Rivera. He may be interested to know Sophie Barrister-
Scoville has taken an interest in politics. She's preparing to run for
his seat in the 2204 election. And oh, boy, is there some dirty
laundry she's got to shove in a closet first."

With business out of the way, it was finally time to collect his
reward. He pulled up his secure communication line and punched
in his boss's number. Forget the commission! After landing a deal
this big, he was on track to join the board of directors.

The face of Ancestry Data Conglomerate's president Adeline
Zhang materialized on his hologram viewer, and Malcolm greeted
her with the first genuine smile he'd worn all day. "Good news,
Ms. Zhang! The Barrister-Scoville account is locked in. My
assistant is processing her Platinum membership right now. She'll
be an exceptionally lucrative customer."

The president spit out a harsh laugh. "Don't get sentimental on
me, Turlington. You know as well as I do—Sophie Barrister-Scoville isn't the customer. She's the *product*."

original story concept by John Graham
first published in Ancestry Data Conglomerate, *by John Graham*
et. al.

WINTER GARDENING

LILLIAN ANGELOVIC

He stands in the bedroom doorway,
No sapling easily pushed aside.
Wide trunk and branches,
Thick fists outstretched,
Balding not from age but chosen season,
Puffed up now under snow and cold anger.

All growth is seasonally affected.
Only thin twigs protrude from grey flesh,
Unwelcoming to leaves, songbirds, and exits.
The bark bark bark,
Scratchier now—
Demanding explanations for the dirt under my nails.

I wave wilted flowers from the window precipice.
Seeing no fire escape
Or knotted bedsheets,
My petals close tight at the 12-story drop,
Where rooted trees cannot follow
And icy concrete welcomes.

GRAVITY

G.R. GOODMAN

I am the endless rain where hapless drown.
My only melody, the winsome song
That Sirens sing before they drag you down,
Into the depths, where mortals don't belong.

I visit in the quiet of the night,
When loneliness enshrouds you like a tomb
My cruel melancholy will ignite,
The smoldering of charcoal tempered gloom.

From here, not even photons can escape.
Dark matter's pull allows but constant night.
Impossible to draw back on the drape,
To force the hidden demons into light.

Grim tidings from the depths of hell arise.
The mind, like tilting earth, begins to spin,
Until a wobble signals its demise.
Destruction of the man comes from within.

ONE OF THEM

MONICA J. WILLIAMS

F ive years ago, an envelope arrived unexpectedly in my university mailbox. I saw it as I glanced into the mailroom on my way to the communal kitchen at the end of the hall. Usually, my brief glances toward the cubby holes yielded only emptiness. When mail did appear, it tended to arrive not as a small envelope resting quietly on the particleboard shelf but as glossy advertisements from academic publishers.

Curious, I swerved into the fluorescent-lit room and picked up the cream-colored interloper. On the front, my name and campus address. On the back, police department insignia. *Probably a thank-you note*, I thought, as I slid my finger through the gap at the top of the envelope. *Another piece of evidence for my tenure file.*

Recently, a dozen students and I had finished a research project on public opinion of the local police department. Over a few years, we'd designed, implemented, and analyzed results from a door-to-door survey. While most people supported the department, our findings revealed concerning (and expected) differences in opinions between neighborhoods and racial and ethnic groups. This, I thought, would spur conversations about racial and socioeconomic inequalities in police-community relations.

At first, I'd felt exhilarated at the potential for my work to positively impact local communities. After submitting written reports and presenting our findings, the conversations I'd hoped for never materialized. Law enforcement administrators and city council members applauded the broad public support and then ignored the issue of differences in support between communities within the city. Still, I'd take the thank you.

Inside the envelope, the ivory cardstock felt too formal for a simple note, but then the police department often outdid my casual academic style. Pulling out the paper, I found not a thank-you note but an invitation to the department's annual celebration and awards ceremony. I imagined tedious speeches and awards going to people I'd never met. *Nope,* I thought, *no need to go.*

On my way to the recycling bin, I scanned the rest of the invitation. Time, date, place. And then I stopped. How had I missed it the first time? At the top, the reason for inviting me. They were awarding me a Certificate of Merit. A pang of indecision followed a flicker of pride.

Had I really done enough to warrant an award? Academics aren't accustomed to public recognition of our work. Publications, tenure, and the occasional university award—nods to the daily sprints of research and teaching—are supposed to sustain us. Although the research with my students had taken years of work, the time we spent constructing the survey, recruiting and training volunteers, knocking on doors, and entering and analyzing data felt so ordinary, just part of the job, nothing that warranted a Certificate of Merit. Rather than toss the invitation in the recycle bin, I took it to my office to consider my next move.

In my office, I dropped into my desk chair and turned toward the window. As a feminist sociologist in a competitive profes-sional field, I knew that my tendencies to overachieve and under-estimate my efforts contributed to questioning whether I deserved the award. But somehow, this particular situation felt different.

As I looked down upon the fountain raining into the goose-dominated duck pond, I realized that my internal debate over accepting the award came less from thinking I didn't deserve it than from uncertainty about the implications of doing so. The decision felt as weighty as accepting a marriage proposal.

My people-pleasing self has always been more of a change-from-within activist. I want to upend unjust systems, and yet I want to stay safe in my white, middle-class, cisgender female box. The people I worked with at the police department seemed genuine in their desires to use research to improve policing, but they were also so steeped in police culture that they often defaulted to dangerous us-versus-them, good-versus-evil mentalities. Still, I believed in the importance of collaboration between researchers and law enforcement to bring about desperately needed institutional reforms.

But how to reconcile this belief with the immense grief of knowing that many more people would die before anything changed? If I wanted my "us" to be people advocating against brutality and other police violence, could I really accept an award from the institution facilitating the harm? A swarm of criticisms invaded my brain. The loudest derided me for being just another white person ineffectively raging against the machine. The thought of having to choose between my tendency toward change-from-within activism and radical social justice reform roiled my insides. I craved a quick resolution, but I knew I shouldn't rush to an answer.

With an exasperated sigh, I swiveled back toward my desk, shoved the invitation aside, and tried to resist the urge to continue analyzing the situation. I left the office knowing full well that, despite my efforts to move on, my brain would continue to mull the issue until I'd reached a final decision.

When I returned the next morning, the invitation still sat on my desk, insisting upon an answer. After hanging my backpack on the hook behind the door, I plunked into my chair and reached down to start the computer. I had only a few minutes before teaching my first class of the day, but I knew I wouldn't be able to concentrate on anything else until I responded to the invitation.

I opened my email and, despite not knowing what to say, began a response. In the first few attempts, I thanked the department for the invitation but graciously declined. Yet, no matter how I wrote it, the refusal felt wrong. Finally, after multiple rephrasings, I thanked the department and then said that I'd attend the banquet with my husband. Before I could change my mind, I typed my name, sent the email, and hurried off to class.

As predicted, the resolution quieted my anxious brain. I still wondered whether I'd made the right choice, but that debate ran in the background. Unfortunately, not long after, a new problem arose that sent me right back into deliberation.

Compared to the gravity of people dying, my new problem sounds so frivolous that I hesitate to put it in writing. To do so risks casting myself as a stereotypical woman who spends too much time on inconsequential decisions. And yet, the new issue is what makes this story less about my internal conflicts than about the struggles of a cisgender white woman to prove herself within the confines of a hyper-masculine, patriarchal institution. I must get it down, so here goes.

In the days before the banquet, I realized that I had nothing to wear. My brain morphed this new concern into an obsession with finding the right outfit for the occasion. As a woman, a professor, and a person who's always wanted to fit in, I'd become accustomed to the uneasiness that trickled through my body when I walked into a room full of police administrators in uniform. To counteract my obvious out-of-placeness, I usually met these men wearing what I think of as my "Dr. Williams armor": gray or black slacks, rayon shirts beneath knit cardigans, and slip-on Clarks. Tucked safely into this suit, the anxious people-pleasing girl morphed into Dr. Williams, a calm and collected woman who spoke confidently in her expertise as a researcher and policing scholar.

Now, suddenly, Dr. Williams would have to forego her trusty

armor for a dressier outfit, one that threatened to expose her as just another woman trying to make it in a man's world. As I surveyed my closet, I saw that no matter what dress or pants-and-shirt combination I found, the shoes would give me away. Almost half of women own high heels, but I was not one of them. Trail runners, snow boots, sport sandals, flip-flops, a pair of sensible flats—none of these would work. Dr. Williams, I decided, needed a pair of heels.

As kids, my sister and I were forbidden from wearing any shoe taller than the three-quarter-inch heels of patent-leather Mary Janes. Still, playing dress-up on hot Florida afternoons taught me the power of high heels. Our dress-up box held garish frocks that puddled around our feet, and sparkly-fake strings of pearls, clip-on earrings, bracelets, and rings. We'd start our trans-formation from girls to ladies by donning the gowns and jewelry, but only when I slipped on the heels was my transformation complete. In those tall, sloping shoes, I felt sophisticated, older, respectable. Like the three-quarters of women who say heels hurt their feet, I could never wear them for more than a few minutes. And yet, I always chose the heels because even then, I knew they marked the pinnacle of looking good.

Today, I cringe at how much that young me reveled in the misplaced confidence boost of a pair of shoes. But I cannot fault her for internalizing societal messages that high heels boost women's status and make us more attractive to men. After all, even after years of sociological training and a resulting Ph.D., I still allowed the looming male gaze of a police banquet to send me shopping for a pair of the very same shoes in which I'd found confidence as a child.

In the dressing room of a generic retail clothing store, I tried on pants and a rayon shirt that the saleswoman helped me pick out. As I stood in front of the mirror, she affixed a too-sparkly necklace around my neck and a matching bracelet around my wrist. Then, she opened a shoebox containing a pair of heels so tall that I began to laugh.

"No," I said. "No way I could walk in those."

She pulled them from the box with a smile. "Just try them."

Feeling compliant, I sat on a padded bench and slid my foot through the ankle straps into the open-toed black leather at the top of the shoe. On my feet, the chunky cork-colored block heels seemed slightly less ominous than they had when lying in their tissue-paper in the box. As the saleswoman buckled the strap, my outer ankle bone prickled with the memory of being fitted for stiff Mary Janes at JCPenney's as a girl. Those shoes rubbed my skin raw no matter what adjustments the salesman made. I hoped these wouldn't do the same.

With both shoes on, I took a breath, unfolded from the bench, and appraised the three-and-a-half-inch-taller version of myself in the mirror. Simply standing on my own two feet felt like a major accomplishment. As when I was a kid, I felt more grown-up and sophisticated than I had just moments before. Liking what I saw, I bought the entire ensemble.

Unfortunately, when I returned home and showed the outfit to my mom over video chat, she confirmed my suspicion that despite the heels and sparkly jewelry, the pants and shirt weren't dressy enough. So much for heels making the outfit. I stowed the accessories in my closet and went searching for a dress.

In the fitting room at another chain clothing store, I examined a stretchy black dress with a gold zipper up the back. The fabric hugged my body without being too tight, and when I checked over my shoulder in the mirror, I saw no unseemly hip bulges or underwear lines. Imagining the finished look with the heels and jewelry, I decided that yes, this dress would work. Still, just to be safe, I texted a picture to my mom. She agreed and finally, I had something to wear.

The evening of the banquet, I curled my hair (something I very rarely do), zipped myself into the dress, squeezed a layer of tinted lip gloss onto my usually makeup-free face, and contorted my feet into the unnatural shape of the heels. When I stepped in front of the mirror for one last assessment, I saw myself not as Monica, the 39-year-old academic going to a banquet to receive an award, but as Monica, a girl desperately hoping that wearing just the right shoes would help her pass as a respectable human being.

My husband Matthew parked our car down the sidewalk from the entrance to the banquet hall. I sat for a moment, preparing for the long walk to the door. Although I wasn't in danger of tumbling off the chunky heels, I gripped the car door to steady myself. Matthew waited on the sidewalk with an arm offered in my direction. As I stepped up next to him, I smiled at our suddenly equal height. I liked being able to meet his eyes without having to crane my neck upward. Intertwining my arm in his, I let him support me in a tiptoe toddle to the door.

Inside, I waved to a couple of people I'd worked with but otherwise stayed close to Matthew. Amid deep-voiced men in starched uniforms, I felt like a beacon, drawing attention to the body I usually hid behind pants and professional shirts. By the time we reached our table at the front of the room (a place mandated by name cards), the balls of my feet ached. I slid into my chair and, in a subtle act of defiance, slipped off my shoes beneath the floor-length tablecloth.

Consider the woman walking barefoot down the sidewalk, a pair of heels dangling from her fingers. She's a wild one, we're told. If it's still dark outside, she's probably had too much to drink. By shedding her shoes, she signals her disregard for social norms and puts herself in even more danger of becoming a victim. If it's morning, she's on a "walk of shame." Respectable women, we're told, keep their shoes on. To defy this convention means rejecting the very femininity that supposedly protects us in this dangerous world. Maybe, like me, her feet pulse red where leather straps pushed against the knuckles of her toes. Maybe she wants to give herself an opportunity to flee from a threatening person. Maybe she just likes the feel of the cool concrete against her skin. No matter her reasons, the dangling heels are a liability. On her feet, they're a different kind of liability, one that requires propping up, help moving through the world, and constant vulnerability. Knowing all of this, I wriggled my unrestrained toes and let them breathe.

As we awaited the start of the ceremony, I studied the program on the table in front of me. On the front, a photocopied image of a police badge. Across the top of the shield, I could just make out the word "Patrolman." I knew at least one officer who'd advocated for and received an "Officer" badge, but apparently the "Patrolman" legacy persisted. No one heard me groan above the din of hearty greetings filling the room.

The ceremony began in militaristic style: Master of Ceremonies, Honor Guard, and Welcome Address from the chief, a military veteran. Dinner arrived, and we ate while watching a video tribute to the department. Soon, the chief introduced the guest speaker, a colonel in the military. I took a breath and braced for war stories.

The colonel spoke of the strength and bravery of "men in uniform."

And women, I thought.

Men willing to fight when duty called.

Fight whom?

Keeping our streets safe.

Against what and for whom?

The speech began to feel interminable. His words encapsulated everything I taught my students about the problems with police culture. To vent the antipathy growing in my chest, I rolled my eyes and fiddled with the white linen tablecloth. I wondered what the few policewomen in the room thought about all this. When the colonel finally finished, I neither clapped nor looked up, a covert protest of his characterization of police as heroic angelmen who are the only reason our cities don't dissolve into chaos.

Finally, we arrived at the presentation of awards. Commendations for bravery and lifetime achievements went to tall, brawny men who'd rushed into headlong into dangerous situations.

Acceptance speeches, jokes, and other commentaries reinforced the idea of good officers as strong men who control any situation at any cost, human or otherwise.

As the masculine bravado thickened, I began to realize the irony of my situation. I'd dressed my body in unfamiliar clothes to blend in with a group of people whose foundational values directly contradicted my own. What exactly was I trying to fit into? Why did I care so much what these people thought? What was I doing there?

Before I had time to fully process these questions, the presenter called my name. I slid my feet into their claustrophobic cells and rose from my seat. Approaching the stairs to the stage, I felt more exposed than ever. Shoes on. Dress tight. Jewelry glinting. The heels and the dress and the jewelry that secured my cisgender femininity also threatened to make a fool of me.

Don't fall. Don't fall. Don't fall, I commanded myself as I neared the stairs.

First step. *Slow down.* Second step. *Focus.* Third step. *Almost there.*

Relieved, I took the final step and plodded across the stage. With every eye fixed upon my body, I wanted to appear strong, willful, smart—all the characteristics the speakers before me had lauded as hallmarks of a good person. My stunted gait ensured I was none of these.

I made it to the presenter, took the plaque, and smiled toward a shadowed audience. Then, I picked my way back to the stairs where I clung to the railing and stepped sideways to ensure that my long, unnaturally curved feet fit solidly on each step. It occurred to me that if I needed to, I could neither run nor jump away from danger.

By the time I reached our table, my transformation was complete. Constantly afraid of falling, I could only concentrate on remaining upright in a world that insists upon seeing women as fragile and weak. I'd become dependent, first upon my husband and then upon the railing, to move. The heels had done me no favors. In a room reeking of machismo, I'd become that little girl playing dress-up with her sister in the heat of a Florida afternoon.

After enduring the rest of the banquet, I left with an overpowering desire to wash the unabashed display of exclusive, masculine camaraderie from my body. At the same time, I knew that I'd never be able to scrub hard enough to reach the disgust I felt for letting my need to be liked muffle my activist voice. I'd been too polite. I hadn't pushed them when they focused on the parts of our research that made them look good. I'd cloaked myself in traditional femininity to attend a banquet that legitimized the entire organization.

Five years later, as I berate myself for these failures, a friendlier voice arises. This one reminds me that despite wanting to save the world, I am only one person acting within unequal social systems and structures. Sometimes, my desire to be liked overpowers my urge to upend patriarchal systems. And that's okay. Sometimes, it's all just so damn exhausting that I can't force myself to ignore a lifetime of messages telling me that I must dress and behave in ways that serve unequal power structures. And that's okay, too. Sometimes, the voice whispers, I can only be a flawed human being doing the best she can.

WHEN THE BOUGH BREAKS

BRYAN YOUNG

held her hand, cold and clammy, wishing I could transfer the breadth of my warmth to her. Her skin was pale and sweaty, and all of the vibrant life she had had, even just a day, before had gone. "It's all right, my love. The doctor is coming."

"I'm scared, Daddy," she said weakly.

"The doctor is coming," I repeated.

She'd fallen so ill so suddenly after dinner the night previous, I couldn't imagine any sort of infection would have had the time to set in. I spent an entire sleepless night trying everything I could to soothe her stomach and cease her vomiting. Fortunately, it stopped on its own, but only because there was nothing left in her stomach to heave. I knew I had to keep some nourishment in her or risk causing permanent damage, so I had seltzer crackers and water on hand, but she could only nibble or sip the barest of portions.

I was truly worried.

I couldn't lose her.

Three heavy knocks beat against the front door, and my wife, little Ellie's stepmother, opened the door and admitted the doctor. Muted through the wood, they spoke in solemn tones fit for the somber occasion as she led him into the bedroom.

"Doctor Roosevelt," I said, looking up to him as he entered, but not letting go of Elli's hand. I wanted her to know that I would be there every step of the way. She made no move to let me go anyhow, so standing would have been futile. "Thank God you're here."

"I rushed over as soon as I got your message. Now let's see, shall we? How are you feeling, Eleanor?"

She mumbled a response as weak as her pulse, then coughed and repeated louder. "I don't feel well."

"Let's see what we can do about it."

"Thank you, Doctor," she said, precocious as ever despite her sickness.

If Doctor Roosevelt could do nothing for her malady, then I didn't know what hope I could have left, save for faith in God that he wouldn't take another dear loved one from me. Eleanor's mother died in childbirth, along with our would-be son. We'd chosen the name Elliot, and that's what was marked on the grave beside Victoria's. I visit it often and I'd be damned if I had to suffer the pain of ordering another child-sized coffin and grave-stone for Eleanor. I hoped there would be many years yet before she joined her mother and brother.

Doctor Roosevelt made his examination, listened to her wheezing breath, asked her where it hurt, and felt around her stomach to see what the matter might be with her insides.

She winced every time he touched her stomach.

"For pity's sake," I muttered.

"I'm so sorry, Eleanor," the doctor said to her upon my utterance.

No one liked seeing a child in any pain, let alone mortal.

"Can you tell me when you started feeling this way, Eleanor?" he asked her finally.

She nodded her little head. "After dinner. We ate and I readied for bed..." Ellie coughed again and paused, holding her stomach as though to keep in what little of its contents may have been left. "Brushing my hair in the mirror, it all came up again."

The doctor looked around the room as if searching for an answer before casting his gaze on me. "Did anyone else at dinner suffer any similar malady?"

I shook my head. "It was just my wife and me, and Eleanor, of course. Elizabeth and I are fine, as you saw."

"Hmmm." Doctor Roosevelt tilted his head, lost in thought. I couldn't imagine holding the power of life or death in my hands as he did. And I imagine he too grew weary of birthing children only to have them die so young. He'd known Ellie all her life and surely didn't want to see her in a grave any more than I did.

The good doctor lifted his black medical bag onto his lap with the weight of carried bricks and withdrew a vial full of a milky white substance. "It's very important that you drink all of this as soon as you can, Eleanor. Do you understand?"

"I understand, Doctor Roosevelt." She struggled to raise her arm but accepted the dose of medicine and brought it to her lips.

Then, gravely, the Doctor looked to me. "May I speak with you outside for a moment?"

"Of course." I turned to Ellie and brought her hand to my mouth, kissing her soft skin gently. "I will be back in just a moment, my love. I will be here for you."

She coughed again. "Thank you, Daddy."

In the hallway outside Ellie's room, the doctor made sure the door was closed behind us and looked around for anyone else that might be listening. Satisfied, he whispered to me. "Do not be alarmed when I tell you that I think she might have ingested some poison by mistake. I'm sorry to say that it could be fatal. I don't want to offer false hope, but if she consumed what I suspect, the compound I gave her will help as long as she doesn't ingest any more of this poison."

"How would she have ingested it?" I asked. I truly had no idea.

"It's everywhere. From rat poison to food poison, it could be absolutely anywhere. I've seen this before, and it's never good."

"I don't think she'd mistake poison for something worth eating."

"She seems a bright girl and always has been. It's worth considering that," he got in closer and lowered his voice further, "perhaps it was administered to her."

"What are you suggesting?"

"I've seen it before. Don't let her take anything you haven't prepared for her yourself. Ensure the safety of every ingredient. It would be wise to prepare your own food and drink as well. For her part, make sure she drinks lots of water after my concoction. With luck, she'll pass this quickly and it won't be an issue again as long as you're vigilant."

"I'll make sure my wife and I are nothing but careful."

The doctor looked back and forth down the hallway once more and narrowed his eyes. "Perhaps it's better if you both only prepare your own food."

"What are you implying, Doctor?"

"I'm just asking you to be cautious if you wish your daughter to see another year. Seven is far too young to die. As is your thirty-and-seven."

"Agreed."

"I'll come to check in the morning. I pray she makes it through the night."

"Thank you, Doctor."

Roosevelt left as quickly as he came, leaving me dazed. I stood there by myself, outside Ellie's door, wondering how to proceed.

Taking a deep breath, I went back in to see my beautiful daughter. Her sallow skin and darkened eyes left her a ghost of her former self. No laughter or cheer was writ on her features, just the sadness of the indignity of her infirmity. I saw the dram of medicine half-drank and smiled at her. "Doctor Roosevelt says you must drink all of it."

"I know. It just tastes so bad."

"My darling, it is imperative you finish."

"He says I'm going to die, doesn't he? That's why you went out to talk?"

My heart broke, but the facade of my warm smile had to stay

true. "Hush, dear. He said no such thing. Drink your medicine and we'll get through this. We'll be back in the park in no time."

She collapsed back into her pillows. "I feel as if I'm dying."

Guilt worked to betray my smile. "My love, you are but seven years old and have not experienced as much as I. Trust when I say that if you were dying, we would surely know it."

"Will you sit with me, Daddy?"

"In a moment, my sweet. Give me a moment. Finish your medicine while I speak with your mother."

She nodded her head and sipped at the vial. I quietly prayed for its efficacy as I left the room in search of my wife.

"How is she?" Elizabeth asked.

"The doctor thinks she can pull through. He gave her a dose of medicine, and I'm to monitor her food and drink carefully."

Elizabeth nodded. "I'm so sorry you're going through this. It must be dreadfully difficult to have lost so much and risk losing it all again."

I nodded, unable to form words, unable to fathom what I would do if I lost Ellie, too.

"But it won't be so bad," Elizabeth said. "You'll see. No matter how it turns out."

"Won't it? My heart lays in that room, pale as a sheet and dying."

"Grief feels deadly, but rarely is, my love. You will live on, and everything between us will be right."

"I will not bury her, too."

"I will help however I can. What are we to be looking for as we keep her fed, then? What instructions did the doctor give?"

"He suggested I alone prepare her food and ensure its purity."

"It's purity?" she said, her voice raising a single, surprised octave.

"Something she ate disagreed with her. I am to assure it doesn't happen again."

"I can help."

"He was clear, this is my duty."

Her cheeks flushed with uncalled-for sternness. "This is my duty, and I will help."

"It will be alright, my love. I can take this burden on my own until she makes it out of the worst."

She twisted her kerchief in a knot between her hands. "No. I insist that I will be helping."

I furrowed my brow and tried ignoring my most uncharitable thoughts. "Do not concern yourself with it, darling. I will take on this burden. She is my child, and I will nurse her to health."

"When we married, she became my child, too, and I will see this finished to the end of her days."

My heart stopped, for the briefest of moments. A set my jaw tight. "She will outlive us both."

"One prays for that, but it is not always so."

"I must return to her."

"Of course," she said. Was that a knife's edge to her voice? "Let me know how I can help."

"Yes, love," I said absently.

All I knew for certain was that I needed to get back to my beloved Eleanor before anything else happened to her. And if these were her final days, I wanted to be there for every second of them.

I found Ellie in bed, just as I'd left her, the entirety of the Doctor's dram consumed. "That's a good girl," I told her. "And I won't find the contents of this in the planter, will I?"

"No, Daddy. I took it. Every drop. It tasted awful, like chalk and castor oil."

I lifted the empty vial and stared at it, praying with every fiber of my body that it would work. "Perhaps that's what it was."

"What's wrong, Daddy?"

"Nothing."

"You look sad."

"It's just that I don't like seeing you ill."

"It's something else, I know it."

"No, my love. Your weakened state has rattled me, is all."

She closed her eyes. "I'm just so tired."

"I know, my love."

"I just want to sleep."

"I'll be right here, my love."

I gripped her tiny hand and wished that I could transfer my constitution to her. Surely, I could have withstood the poison in her stead.

"Get your rest, my love."

She faded to sleep, and I kept checking her breathing to make sure that the worst had not come. I couldn't bear it, but if she did go in her sleep, I would be there holding her hand. She would meet the other side knowing how much I loved her here, feeling the warmth of my hand, ushering her to a better life.

As morning gave way to afternoon, I found myself dozing as well. When color returned to Ellie's cheeks, it felt safe to nap. Perhaps we *would* make it together.

The opening of the door awoke me, and then that was followed by Elizabeth with a tray for tea. "Wake up, it's time for you both to have some tea."

With a start, I woke, not expecting the intrusion. Elizabeth had shown no interest in sitting with Ellie and had been forbidden from helping keep her hunger and thirst sated.

Ellie opened her eyes halfway and licked her lips. "I think I could drink some tea."

Panic and paranoia hit me equally. I didn't know what to say to avert their suspicion. "The doctor said no tea for a few days, love, if you remember."

Ellie hung her head. "I don't remember, Daddy. You spoke outside the room."

"So we did." I looked to Elizabeth, unsure of how to read her expression. "You can leave the tray; I'll drink both teas."

"No, you can't," she said hurriedly. "I'll bring it back when you're both ready."

She left, and realization dawned on me.

I lifted Ellie up out of the bed, gathering all of her blankets with her.

"Where are we going, daddy?" she asked.

"Somewhere safe, my love. And quiet, for you to recover. The country perhaps."

With her arms wrapped around my neck and the weight of her in my arms, I opened the door as quietly as I could and crept through the hallway.

"Are we telling Elizabeth?" she asked.

"Shhh, my dear." I made sure Elizabeth was nowhere to be seen, then crossed toward the front door and opened it quietly as well, hoping not to alert anyone. "We'll deal with her later. We need to get you well first."

"Yes, daddy."

"No one will ever hurt you again." I closed the door behind us and carried her toward the stable where the carriage awaited.

"Daddy?" she said, settling into the carriage where I sat her.

I ceased my haste and looked into her beautiful eyes, hoping I still had many years to look into them. "Yes, Ellie?"

"I love you more than anything."

"I love you more than anything, too, my sweet."

And I meant it.

ERIK

DENIS FEEHAN

"Where's Erik?" Sharon asks.
"I thought you had him," I say.
But my wife does not have
our little boy.
Poseidon's cousin, who lives in our backyard pool
has claimed him.

I jolt up in a cold sweat,
alone in the bed that once held my whole life.
These nocturnal tortures are
exponentially more painful
than the constant reliving that I endure
during the day.
Getting up,
I take two sleeping pills,
washing them down with the ever present
whiskey on my nightstand.
Slowly, I drift off again.

"Where's Erik?" Sharon asks.
"I thought you had him," I say.

FOUR LISTS

MASHA SHUKOVICH

Belgrade, Yugoslavia, 1998

Here's what you need to know about me:

1. My Name is Vida. I used to hate my name, but I don't anymore.
2. I was born in Yugoslavia, so I'm Yugoslavian, but I'm also Serbian, because everyone here has at least two national identities. And now that the war is coming, who knows what we will all be called once it's over.
3. I am eighteen going on nineteen, and I've never been kissed.
4. I look just like my father, only with long hair. His features are so dark, people have nicknamed him Crni (Black), just like his ancestor on his father's side, Đorđe Petrović (or Black George), the hero of Serbian independence against the Turks.
5. My mother stopped speaking when my baby brother died. I was nine at the time. She hasn't said a word, to

me or anyone else, in nine years. It's like she fell asleep and got lost in a dream. I feed her meals and stories every day, hoping she might wake up.

6. My grandmother hates me and the air that I breathe. I have yet to figure out why.

7. I smell colors, hear shapes, and taste names. I'm not entirely sure that I'm human.

8. I hear voices. They tell me things no one else knows. When I was little, I was afraid of them, but now I can't imagine swimming through the world without them. They function like a sixth sense, and in Serbia, someone like me needs one just to stay alive.

9. I don't have many friends, but some of them are gods, which is a pretty good tradeoff.

10. I've been in love with my best friend, Despot, since the age of seven. He is oblivious to that fact. He is about to flee to America, on a green card he got through the lottery, because being an 18-year-old boy in Yugoslavia right now is like dancing with Death.

11. You may not know it, but everything is alive and has a spirit: chairs, letter openers, saltshakers, soil, irises, walnuts, shoes, washing machines, thimbles, sweet paprika, flowerpots with a hole in the bottom, moon, spatulas, water. Especially water.

12. I like rivers, doorways, silence, Converse shoes, holy basil, stories, lists, and the number 13.

13. My favorite thing in the world, after Despot, is cooking.

FROM VIDA'S COOKBOOK:

Plum slatko to honor all visitors, no matter what they're bringing

Every guest is welcome in a Serbian home and offered slatko, sugary preserves made with plums or other fruits, that sweetens even the bitterest of days and the worst of destinies. It is a great way to turn a foe into a friend; a little sweetness goes a long way.

A spoonful of slatko must always be chased down by a glass of ice-cold water. Don't forget to serve water with slatko; one needs the other to express itself fully.

To make the best slatko, you should always talk to the plums first, the way you would to children: the honey in them will recognize the honey in your voice and will rush to the surface to greet you. If you look closely, you will notice that some of the plums you just spoke to have cried tears of joy: they will appear along the edges and around the stalk in the form of little golden droplets. Once you see them, you will know that the plums have indeed heard you and have agreed to be cooked with sugar and made even sweeter in the process. It's important that you ask first before taking; that is the way of making all things friendlier.

Ingredients:

- 1 kg friendly plums
- 1 kg sugar
- Lemon juice (the sunnier the lemon smells, the better)
- Vanilla
- A handful of rose petals (especially important if you're hiding any bitterness under your tongue)

As with any other recipe, it's always good to compliment your ingredients. Like people, plums will be sweeter and more fragrant if praised than if scolded. Save your swear words for battle; they have no place in the kitchen and have been known to poison the food and make the eater sick.

The words you use as you prepare slatko must be soft and round like the plums. Once tasted, they will banish all ill will and fear, which are one and the same.

———

Belgrade, Yugoslavia, 1985

"You are a bad child, Vida."

My Grandmother, Baba Zora, is in the know.

She spits once, like the words she just uttered are too heavy on her tongue and she must expel them before they burn a hole in it. She doesn't do it out of superstitious fear, like so many babas— grandmothers—do, mock-spitting three times to ward off the evil eye and knocking on the nearest piece of wood to invoke the blessings of the spirits that dwell in it.

No, she isn't calling me bad and worthless so that Death and Misfortune wouldn't hear her praise and take me too soon. She isn't bursting with carefully concealed joy, secretly thinking how lovely and plump my arms are, how long and dark my eyelashes, how endearing my giggle.

She isn't concerned with invisible demons, listening intently. She truly means it.

I am a bad, good-for-nothing child. And bad children grow up to be even shoddier adults, so they must be disciplined before they've had time to grow into their worst selves.

Only bad, very bad little girls enter their grandmother's attic room at the top of the creaky staircase while she's at church and get caught in the act. For no one is to enter Baba Zora's room.

Only bad, very bad little girls are then sent out into the communal garden, wedged between grey pre-war buildings, golden with summer haze, to pick the switch with which they will be punished. And if it is your first time picking the switch that you are to be whipped with,

you too might make the mistake of picking a thin, green one, thinking it would hurt less. But you will soon learn that the thinnest ones hurt the most.

If you are one of these bad, good-for-nothing children, your grandmother may say, her words like spells wishing unspeakable things into being, "Vida, there's a devil in you, black as night, and I will beat it out of you. Now kiss the switch you picked."

And if you're quite as bad as I was back then, quite as bad as I surely still am now, at the age of nineteen, you may refuse to kiss the switch, too. And if your grandmother is anything like Baba Zora, you will sorely regret that choice.

There are five things you might remember later:

1. The way the switch cuts through the air, with a crunch, like through an apple.
2. The whispered swish that always comes before the pain.
3. The way the switch rests in midair for a moment before it splits open the center of your right palm, like a ripe pomegranate from Dalmatian coast.
4. The way the skin rises up, like two pink embankments on each side of a red river.
5. The way Baba Zora smells as she moves in for a second strike, like Dr. Oetker vanilla sugar, dry willow wreaths, angry sweat, and secrets.

FROM VIDA'S COOKBOOK
Creamed spinach to feed your resilience

Pick the most stalwart plant you can find, the one that was forgotten and left uncovered during the winter. The one whose leaves froze and died, but the plant itself survived and grew new, pale leaves in the spring. You will know it by its roots—red like chicken legs and smooth.

Wash the leaves tenderly and briefly boil them in hot, salted water, until their color changes to an unforgiving green. Drain them and chop them up finely. If there is a song waiting in your throat to be released, this is the time to do it.

Once chopped up, cook the spinach in butter, and add flour, crushed garlic, and a little Vegeta seasoning. If you are Serbian, like me, you already have your jar of Vegeta handy.

Soothe the spinach with strained milk until it forms a thick, creamy mixture. Let it simmer for a while, until it takes on a resolute shade of pale green.

Serve on a large plate, with two eggs fried sunny side up, like a smile.

————

Belgrade, Yugoslavia, 1998

The boy I love knows many things. Some of them are:

1. How to play upright bass with his 18-year-old forehead furrowed like the waters of the vast ocean he needs to cross to get to America, the land of Brooklyn Spearmint gum, Levi's 501s, and his wildest dreams.
2. How to fill out a Diversity Lottery application in English that he learned by watching Johnny Bravo on Cartoon Network and become one of the 696 people from Yugoslavia to get a green card that most boys our age waiting in line to be drafted into the war they never asked for would gladly give an eye, a hand, or a kidney for.
3. How to pack all his worldly possessions into one large suitcase and one upright bass case and say goodbye to his weeping mother with only the slightest quiver of his lower lip but no tears.
4. How not to notice things that few others could ignore, like the fact that his best friend, me, is desperately, stupidly, hopelessly in love with him and has been since the day we met in first grade eleven years ago.

He is the one I love, this boy who knows so many things worth knowing and is utterly clueless about other, equally important ones. His name is Despot, but that's not his fault.

He was born in the Belgrade City Hospital on the morning of

May 4, 1980. His mother says that she woke up before sunrise that day because she dreamt that river Sava was singing to her, an impossibly beautiful song, cloaked in longing, but once she woke up, she could no longer remember it. But there was another river, flowing between her legs, and she stumbled out of bed and into the street with an old towel stuffed between her knees.

She was rushed to the hospital in a clunky, vanilla-scented Mercedes taxicab, screaming in the throes of labor, amniotic fluid gushing out of her like water from a broken pipe, in perfect rhythm with the folk music blaring from the ancient radio and the terrified cabbie spitting curses through his tobacco-stained teeth. Despite the labor pains and the humiliation of almost giving birth in a taxi, all she could think of as she was being rolled into the hospital on a metal gurney was the song of the river that stubbornly refused to come back to her.

The same day Despot was born, the beloved president and dictator Josip Broz Tito died. It was only a decade before Yugoslavia was to be dissolved. Some things cannot survive the death of those who created them.

The entire country was in mourning that day, people sobbing and wailing at the top of their voices in the streets and collapsing to the ground in heaps of wordless sorrow.

What followed four days later was the largest state funeral in history, only to be surpassed by that of Pope John Paul II several decades later. Among the mourners queuing to pay their last respects to Tito were 31 presidents, 22 prime ministers, 47 ministers of foreign affairs, six princes, and four kings. And then, there were millions of average Draganas and Dragans grieving in a much less dignified manner, in their homes and in the streets of every city, town, and village in Yugoslavia.

With everyone so wholly enveloped in grief, not a single person rejoiced Despot's birth, except for his mother. She secretly thought that President Tito had gotten too much attention while he was alive and that it was now her son's turn to shine.

It was the end of an era, so Despot's mother refused to bestow upon him one of the popular names that celebrated long-awaited freedom, hard-won peace, and selfless camaraderie, like Slobodan, Vladimir, or Branimir. Instead, she decided to name him after her great- grandfather, Despot Bogdanovic, who was said to have been a stern but kind-hearted man. In a word, it was a travesty of a name, guaranteed to attract unwanted attention and cruel jabs of particularly mean schoolmates. But, as a true Serbian woman, Despot's mother chose her son's name out of spite, and that made it perfectly acceptable in her eyes.

However, what she never acknowledged, even to herself, was the fact that the word despot denotes an emperor or a king with unlimited power; a tyrant. And so, as one despot perished on May 4th, 1980, in the private room on the seventh floor of the Department of Cardiovascular Surgery at the University Medical Centre in Ljubljana, another, much less powerful and highhanded one, was born at the stark and austere maternity ward of the Belgrade City Hospital, devoid of lavish flowers and not nearly as quiet, where his mother shared the room with seven other women. So, in a way, Despot was really named after President Tito. And ever since he opened his eyes and looked around the hospital room, he'd had only one thought: How do I get out of this stinkhole of a country?

Despot never gave his name a second thought until he started first grade at the age of seven years and three months. The teasing and taunting started almost immediately, as having an unusual name turned out to be enough of a reason for him to be singled out by his classmates.

"Hey Despot, was your mother drunk when she named you?" one boy would ask, and before Despot could think of a good retort, another one would supply: "No, she just thought it was a perfect name for a skinny little bastard!"

The only crime that a child could commit in the Belgrade of the late eighties greater than to bear an unusual name was to lack a father. And Despot was guilty of both.

Belgrade, Yugoslavia, 1988

It's the third week of first grade, and even at the age of seven, I am painfully aware of how the unwritten rule of good and bad names works. My father named me Vida, after my grandmother's long-departed friend from youth. Nobody else in the entire first grade is called Vida. A couple of kids in class have grandmothers or great-aunts with that name, but the girls are all called Ana, Marina, Sania. All perfectly lovely and age-appropriate names. Not mine.

When I was barely four, my mother explained that my name meant "eyesight" or "life." She said there once was a Pagan and early Christian deity by the name of St. Vid, the god of battle, fertility, and abundance, which didn't sound too impressive to me. He was also the patron saint of clairvoyants and healers, my mother added, which I liked more.

Whenever I think of my name, I see a whirlwind of luscious green foliage, like a jungle, and angular Cyrillic letters intertwining endlessly, like snakes. It tastes like lemongrass: invigorating, tangy, and with a hint of bitterness. It's fragrant and glossy, with sharp, triangular tips. Perhaps not the most delicious of names, but a name with the flavor one wouldn't easily forget.

There's this boy in my class. He's called Despot. His name is so different than mine: smooth and rounded, like a chocolate truffle coated in cocoa powder, soft and brown. But he is, nevertheless, relentlessly teased for his name, just like me. Why they tease me, I can understand. Fluffy pink, candy floss-flavored girl names are infinitely superior to a green one. So are the powder-blue ones that taste of rosewater and lightly toasted, sugarcoated almonds. But can't the other kids see the potential behind a name such as Despot? All the dark, chocolaty richness

lurking right below its powdery surface. The silky bubbles of joy that slowly melt in my mouth as I taste his name on my tongue.

I wait for recess to let him know how special his name is.

"Hey," I announce to Despot. I pause and click my tongue silently seven times. He is playing cars by himself on the edge of the playground. He looks up at me, pushing his sun-streaked bangs out of his dark eyes.

"Hey," he mutters in response and lowers his gaze back to battered toy cars in front of him.

He has two—a green one and a red one. The red one tastes like gummy bears and the green one like sour apple candy.

"Hey, Despot," I say again, louder this time.

"Yeah?" he responds, without looking up. I'm just this weird girl from his class. The one that's always counting cracks in the pavement. He's willing to tolerate me, for now, because his mother told him to be nice to girls.

"Your name," I start, unsure where I'm going with it. I pause to lick my chapped lips.

The warm wind whips a strand of my bushy dark hair into my eyes. I brush it away like an annoying insect.

"I know your name is brown," I say with more conviction, "but it tastes really good. Like chocolate and stuff. Really, really good."

I can hear someone sniggering in the background.

Despot looks up, confused. "What?"

There is no backing out of it now. I raise my voice: "I said your name is brown, and it tastes like chocolate. And it's better than other names."

This is for the benefit of other kids who are now listening to our conversation, uninvited, but nevertheless intrigued. More kids start laughing. I do my best to ignore them. One of the older boys makes a poor attempt at a wolf whistle.

A couple of girls giggle, and one squeals, loudly enough for everyone to hear, in a grating, sing-song voice: "Weird Vida likes Dorky Despot!"

"I do not!" I yell, not looking at her. I'm clicking my tongue rapidly. Seven. Fourteen.

Twenty-four times.

"Vida likes Despot, Vida likes Despot!" more kids start chanting, nudging each other conspiratorially.

"No, I don't!" I bellow, turning to face our audience, tears of rage in my eyes. "Despot and Vida, boyfriend and girlfriend!" sing the rest of the kids.

One of the older boys shrieks, his voice whiny and high-pitched. He puckers his thin lips into a mockery of a kiss: "Hey guys, look, I'm Vida! You are my chocolate, Despot!"

Then, without warning, the thin-lipped boy pushes me onto Despot, who is swaying on the balls of his feet, unsure where to go and what to do with his hands. Despot is one of the nice boys, and I've never seen him hit a girl or even pull a girl's hair like the rest of them. But he has his limits too.

I stumble when the older boy pushes me, lose my balance, and fall on Despot.

And Despot does the only logical thing for a seven-year-old boy in his situation: he pushes me away with as much power and as far as he can, to distance himself from me, the freak.

All that drivel about his name—it's not his fault that Weird Vida decided to pick on him today. I land on my hands, my palms and knees scraped and protesting in pain. The burning feeling in them is a bright, angry, painfully tart orange.

The bell shrills across the schoolyard, announcing the end of recess. It sounds like a box of sewing needles landing on a tin roof: silvery, salty, prickly. Everyone rushes towards their classrooms, Despot among them, their laughter and shouts fading in the distance. I'm alone. But that's nothing new.

———

Belgrade, Yugoslavia, 1998

"I'm sorry," eighteen-year-old Despot whispers softly into my almost nineteen-year-old left ear, and I feel like no time has passed at all since that brittle, green September day, eleven years ago.

We are both lying on his bed, fully dressed. Despot's upright bass is clad in its hard black case that lies open on the floor to show its smooth, mahogany body. It looks like a pharaoh resting in his sarcophagus, the slumbering wearer of the crown, wordlessly obeying the will of the gods. His tall black suitcase with a vertical red stripe, all packed and ready, is waiting, stiff and silent, by the door. It reminds me of a prison guard watching our every move.

Not a single part of me is touching Despot, but I feel like I own the darkness in the room and its many-fingered hands, each of them caressing his face, his hair, his lips, the soft hollow at the base of his throat. I get to touch him in my mind the way I never have in reality.

"I'm sorry," Despot repeats, his brown eyes on mine. "Sorry for what?" I ask.

"For pushing you away in first grade." "That's okay. I don't even remember it," I lie.

He takes my left hand and gently places it over his heart. I gasp and instantly regret it. Did he hear it? My face feels hot and prickly, a swarm of fiery, red bees buzzing through my every pore. I can hear Despot's heartbeats in the tips of my fingers. They match my own.

"I'm sorry anyway," Despot whispers into the dark, my hand on his chest, his hand on mine. A siren bawls in the distance, like a lost cow. It's the loneliest, most beautiful sound.

"We'll stay friends, all right?" he says softly. "Even though I'm leaving for America tomorrow. Even though everyone will say I'm just a gutless draft dodger. Even if I end up becoming a famous jazz player in New Orleans and forget how to speak Serbian and decide never to come back to this dump of a town for as long as I live. Except maybe to have one of your pljeskavica with kajmak. God, I'm gonna miss those! You know, I might die out there, without you to feed me. Still better than dying in someone else's war."

He chuckles at his own bad jokes, like he's apologizing not just for what he said but for who he is, and turns his head to the side to look at me. His face is serious and beautiful, like the moon reflected in still water. There is nothing I want to do more in this world than to press my lips to his.

"We'll stay friends forever, no matter what, Vida," he says with conviction. He has no clue. I've never been anything more than a friend to him.

This thought is too big, too painful to swallow whole, and I can feel bitter tears rolling from the corners of my eyes into the curved shells of my ears.

He's leaving, and it's too late to tell him that I love him. It's too damn late.

"Friends forever, no matter what," I repeat in a whisper, my hand still resting on his chest.

There's a tiny hole in his white t-shirt, right below his collar-bone, and my pinky finger has found it, by total chance, in the dark. The place where my skin is touching his feels like it's been set on fire, a sweet agony I never want to end.

"Can you stay over tonight?" he asks. "Please. It's my last night."

I shake my head no, my throat too dry to speak. It's better to keep silent; I don't want him to hear the tears in my voice.

"Your Dad would totally freak, right?" he chuckles. "And Baba Zora would probably shoot me dead."

I nod, with a fake little laugh. As he shifts his body upward into a sitting position, I inhale the smell of him: Ajax laundry detergent, Brooklyn spearmint gum, and that sunshiny scent of his skin that makes my head spin like I'm riding on a bright yellow merry-go-round under indigo summer skies.

When Despot isn't looking, I put my pinky finger in my mouth, like I used to do with cookies stolen from my grandmother's pantry when I was little. My finger tastes faintly of chocolate truffles dipped in cocoa powder. And precious secrets never spoken.

The rest is a blur: Despot walking me home through the dark, empty, freshly-hosed streets of Belgrade, with only a few drunkards and a stray yellow dog sniffing around trash bins to keep us company. Me crying openly but still saying nothing. Despot balancing on one foot to avoid puddles as he walks next to me: tall, lanky, and awkward, his hands buried deep in the pockets of his jeans.

The ten-minute walk from his mother's apartment to Baba Zora's house has never been so short. I hate the wet streets. I hate the moon staring hungrily from the sky. I hate Despot for leaving. I hate myself for being such a miserable coward. I hate the neighborhood babas peeking through the window curtains to see who is walking home so late at night. They'll be giving a full report about my nighttime dalliances to Baba Zora in the morning.

As we enter the shadows of my doorway, Despot unexpectedly hugs me, and I am so surprised I hardly return the embrace. "Okay, it's time to go," he says and chuckles awkwardly. "I'll see you, mala!"

I am visibly shuddering now: a combination of cool night air and frayed nerves. Despot turns around to leave, and then he seems to change his mind. He is so close to me I can feel his mint-scented breath on my cheek. He leans down, smiles, and shrugs off his denim jacket. He folds it neatly in half and hands me the dark blue bundle.

"Here," he says, "I want you to have it. I know how much you love it. I'll get another one in America. They don't call it the land of denim for nothing."

This is one of Despot's prized possessions: his Levi's 501 denim jacket, a rare and precious original in the land of knockoffs. His cousin brought it for him from America a few years back, for his 16th birthday. I know people who would sell their own mother to get their hands on that jacket. I am so shocked, I can't find my voice. Despot smiles at me, his face briefly illuminated by a street-lamp like a fresco of a medieval saint, but before I can take another breath, he is walking away.

"Thank you!" I yell after him, stupidly.

"I'll see you!" he shouts back. He doesn't turn around, just waves his hand, his t-shirt eerily white in the light of the moon.

"I love you," I whisper to his wide shoulders and slim frame as they dissolve into the night, and I hug the Levi's denim jacket to my chest like a drowning girl grasping a lifeline. The sweet scent of Despot that still lingers on the jacket hugs me back and walks me through the door, holding me tightly in its tantalizing grip as I stumble into my bed, where I am finally free to howl my sorrow into the pillow, the busybody neighbors and Baba Zora be damned.

Tomorrow, I will do four things:

1. Get up before sunrise and before Baba Zora.
2. Go to church and light four candles: one for Despot's safe journey, one for his dreams to come true, and one for him not to forget me. The fourth one I will light for the dead. It's always good to remember the dead.
3. Make chocolate truffles.
4. Eat them.

Four is a good number: not too big and not too small. Four is green. It smells like apples.

I can do four.

FROM VIDA'S COOKBOOK
Chocolate truffles to help you endure your beloved's leaving

Note to the cook:
First, always think about the one who feeds your heart. Once

you can see their eyes clearly, commence your work. If your true love is not to be found, you can try to substitute the next best thing for it. But it will never taste the same.

Method:

Mix bitter chocolate and sweet cream and let them come together hastily, like unlikely lovers. Add their illegitimate child, the vanilla sugar, and allow it to stand for a few minutes, muddled, until it accepts its destiny. Stir until smooth. Taste the mixture. It should taste honest and kind and brown all over. It should feel like smooth jazz wrapped in honey trickling down your throat. If you can still feel the spiky whiteness of sugar crystals piercing your tongue, you need to work it some more. Allow it to cool, then place in the refrigerator to rest for two hours. Once cool, roll in your hands quickly like you do before you peel a hot chestnut from a street vendor, then dip in unsweetened cocoa powder. The truffles should melt in your mouth like forgiving snowflakes. If your beloved leaves without saying goodbye, double the batch. It won't mend your heart, but it will make it easier to carry the broken pieces around.

A GLACIER'S GLIDE

DANIEL MORESCHI

An arctic glacier crawls across a frozen floor,
while waves of steely clouds abound, compound, and pour
their snow onto its lucid bastions, forming streaks
that slowly fortify its crevasses and peaks.

It ventures onwards through a powdered valley where
it's ardently caressed by frets of errant air.
Cacophonies of eerie wheezes backed by wails,
attune with sudden swirls that circle on the trails

as frigid fragments rise again in unison;
revolve, converge, then flit in stintless fits that run
with unseen swoops. The structure still maintains a base,
outlasting hoary dawns whenever they retrace.

Its fronts and sides show signs of tumult-sculpted drapes
with countless layers turned to shattered shards. The scrapes,
meanwhile, reflect a brimming myriad of gleams,
like sun-brushed constellations seized by icy seams.

It navigates a steep meander and suspends
within an unforgiving depth of briny beds,
while treading rocky sinks that rend an inner quake.
A pillar wears expanding fractures. Ridges break

up into rains of milky dust. A sheet erodes
in rows of ruptured roars. An ailing bridge unloads
its decks as walls come crashing down. The remnants stay
to coat an ocean with a crystalline array.

BORN AGAIN

MARIE TOLLSTRUP

Surviving major surgery may be traumatic, not unlike being born on a foreign planet. Nothing is predictable. Nothing is the same. Wrenched back to infancy, I face a state of complete helplessness. Just as a totally defenseless baby experiences cold, hunger, and vulnerability, so too, I, the newly conscious patient, flails in a hospital bed, cold and hungry, not having eaten for forty-eight hours. Just as the shock of light initiates a baby into life on an alien planet that may prove precarious to his/her survival, so too, I survey my unfamiliar surroundings. Both baby and patient are dependent on the mercy of their caregivers for their very existence.

Pain, an unwelcome visitor, moved in and took up residence in my body. I had been lucky for most of my long life to have lived pain free. Areas of my body that had functioned without awareness began announcing their existence, demanding full attention. My body that had taken care of business without conscious promptings on my part, rebelled and screamed at me for making poor choices. Intense abdominal pain did not permit me to move from my frozen semi-prone position. When I tried to alter my body's position, pain spasms racked my gut. I prayed for relief.

Held captive in a hospital room with time on my hands, my mind wandered. I had lived a lucky life up to this point. I was born in America, which is often an overlooked privilege. I was most fortunate that both parents loved and provided for me and my seven siblings. We grew up on a large Wisconsin potato farm where we explored both river and woods to our hearts' content. Luck had steeped my life—my teaching career productive, my marriage happy, my friends devoted, and my life long. I had been blessed with these incomparable, sacred gifts. When autumn leaves announced my eighty-fifth birthday this past November, I was contemplative but anxious. Three of the significant men in my life all died at age eighty-five—my grandfather, my father, and my husband. My own eighty-fifth birthday gave me pause, wondering if I would join their ranks. Would I hear heaven's trumpet calling me home?

Change was in the winter winds. Both Christmas and New Year's stunned me. I had invited two sisters and a brother for the Christmas holidays because I had not seen them during the two prior pandemic years. On Christmas Day, while preparing persimmon pancakes for my family, I felt intense, stabbing pain in my lower abominable area. After removing the first pancake batch from the griddle, I turned off the burner, walked over to the counter, sat, and put my head down on my folded arms waiting for the spasms to pass. When my intense distress persisted, I went to lie down. As most humans do, I procrastinated until 2:00 a.m. when I arrived at the ER. Only later did I discover it was a fortunate arrival hour because I received immediate attention and service.

A prompt CT scan indicated I might have a ruptured bowel. By 7:00 a.m. on December 26th, I was in surgery, which instead revealed I had a gastric bleeding ulcer. Major surgery changed my world and seeped into my psyche to alter my attitude. I was toppled from my smug, independent pedestal. My arrogance never permitted me to contemplate I would grovel for a helping hand. As a former capable adult, I was transformed into reliant infant, totally dependent on others to care for my basic bathroom and nutritional needs. Nurses and their aides became my best friends. As a needy patient, I blessed each eager face who arrived to assist me. When I left the hospital, I casually said to an assisting nurse, "Prior, I had lived a pain-free life, so now it was my turn." Her wiser response was 'not necessarily.'

Discharged from the hospital four days later, I sported a six-inch vertical gash below my breasts, through my bellybutton, to mid-stomach, decorated with seventeen staples. Arriving home with a walker, I had to relearn how to walk, get in and out of bed, sleep in a reclining position, and rise unassisted from the commode. Both my sisters, who had joined me for a holiday visit, changed their casual hats to don instead caregiving attire. Pat, the capable, self-assured driver, ran daily errands, jockeyed between Harmons, Wal-Mart, Costco, and Alpine Medical Supplies. Jeanne, the compassionate, empathetic sister, shadowed me as a nurse. To avoid untimely accidents, I welcomed Depends with a Poise liner for a month. My recovery was delayed due to three additional ER trips, all related to my recent surgery. I needed ER expertise in dealing with both post-surgical fecal impaction and cellulitis in my lower right leg. Lymphedema plagued me for over a year.

I never fathomed the degree of debility I would experience during my immediate recovery. Temporarily detoured, I was depressed and reduced to a defenseless invalid. Because I had lived solo for ten years after my husband's death in 2012, I was forced to face my new reality. Just how independent was I? I had passed through a traumatizing birth canal of pain. I was living in my home, but it transformed into a foreign landscape. It was time for a reset. For the first time at eighty-five, I admitted I was vulnerable and had to relearn simple skills. How do I get from point A to point B without a walker? My top priority became braving independent steps using furniture and walls for support. My goal was to ditch my walker in two weeks and store it in the closet next to the shower bench. Yes, I was determined to stand in the shower to bathe. Yes, I cooked my own quinoa and millet cereal for breakfast. Yes, after two weeks I slid down in bed to sleep prone without extreme abdominal pain. I also had to vanquish my fear of driving. At January's close with Jeanne as passenger, I drove myself to see Dr. Watson, my surgeon. January melted away while I regained my basic independent living skills. My expressed choice was to live solo as I had done the prior ten years.

Then, 2022 galloped on into February. It was time to reintroduce myself to my writing groups and book group. My daily reading habit had evaporated. Although ideas had occurred to me, I had not penned a poem or story since mid-December. Words had been my constant companions. How does one invite these comrades back? How does one string captivating words together that will arrest the reader? Like Steven King after his 1999 tragic accident, I asked similar questions. Do I remember how to write? Am I committed to the writing act? Am I able to write again? I learned after some false starts that it has to do with the rituals of starting over. Most of our lives are spent witnessing beginnings and endings like sunrises and sunsets. I chose to begin each day with a blank page and fill it with confessional words. Each day I read for an hour, making new friends with the characters I met. Slowly, the dance rhythm of beginning again returned, providing comfort and solace, a moving spiritual experience. The act of starting over transformed to resilience.

I was unaware Death hovered over me while my surgeon frantically cleansed me of gastric fluids and staunched my Eliquis-thin bleeding ulcer. During a post-operative visit, my surgeon informed me he had only one chance to go in and do the job right. Yes, Death debated if my time had run its course. Both my surgeon and an ER doctor informed me I was a lucky survivor of my surgery at my advanced age. I was also fortunate during my ordeal that I remained Covid-free. As I entered the normal river of life and felt its rhythm, I kept judging the strength of its current, swimming at a slower pace. I resigned from three boards to ease my stress level, which profoundly had affected my health. Meditation expanded my awareness of the godsend of good health and the priority of maintaining it. Practicing mindfulness grounded me to the moment at hand, and by breathing deeply, I reduced my stress level. Each day proved to be a reflective chance to explore more of the world's mysteries as well as delve within my own soul. I was given the grace to write additional, insightful chapters to my life story.

The best model of beginnings was observing nature during the spring season. Nature was on full display, revealing nascent green, fragile, spreading leaves, and red rosebuds holding promise. Seated before my computer, the immediate large front window proved to be my perfect viewing site. Each day, I witnessed miracles in the slow progression of new growth. Then, as Wendell Berry on his porch, I walked through my front door to experience nature's kiss—taste fresh air, hear birdsong, touch tree bark, smell blooming lilacs, observe Larkspur Park's panorama, feel each footfall on the walking path. Only after my morning walk did I feel renewed, my muscles tingling from my workout. I resolved to walk through nature's cathedral door each day.

Major surgery changed everything because of my new vantage point. There was a BS, before surgery, and an AS, after surgery. I thought I was invincible, that I could go on forever with no recognizable end point. Suffering opened doors to wisdom. Yes, I was vulnerable and learned patience while healing and humility when fragile during recovery. I was grateful for my regained mobility and independence. How fortunate I was not to suffer from dementia. Major surgery also proved to be an ultimate gift—one where I gained a deeper compassion and empathy for the ailing elderly and those who suffer from chronic pain and/or disability. I deeply admired nurses, their aides, and hospital staff who were devoted to my care at all hours of the day and night.

I began to dance different rhythms at a slower pace. I had been born again to embrace more of reality and to sanctify each new day I would be given to live. I had been given a gift, blessed with more days to witness other sunrises. In a word, I was offered redemption, the chance to reset the priorities of my life. In the process, I was introduced to the changed person residing in my aged body. Only over time did I accept this less nimble, wiser, older woman I had become.

TRAIL OF SHADOWS

TERRA LUFT

ictoria stood just outside their cabin door looking out over the deck railing and across the valley. The yard below, framed by trees, took her breath away every time. Such beauty. Could she get used to this being the only place they lived when it came time to retire? She wasn't one hundred percent sure, but for Lance and their grand plans for the golden years, she was willing to give it a try.

The eyesore of that damn school bus just visible over the trees pulled her away from her appreciation of the beauty of the mountain community. It annoyed her that she and Lance hadn't found a more affordable cabin property higher up in elevation. It would have been an even more pristine view, but really, she wished to be further away from the tiny town and Utah farming community just below them. She knew that made her shallow. She could acknowledge the amount of privilege she had, but why not be honest with herself when there was no one else around? She dwelled in the city, always had, and even if she could accept the idea of converting a school bus into a house, she didn't understand someone actually doing it, especially without at least painting it so it didn't look like a damn school bus still. Forget the fact that painting it a non-yellow was required by law, since she knew these neighbors didn't care about such things. One of the many things she didn't understand about the small-town life and people who chose to dwell in such a rural place.

She decided to walk up the road for her morning hike today. Uphill was better to get over with first and reward herself with the downhill on the return. Plus, this way she could avoid feeling sad about all the poverty she glimpsed in the farm lots below them until the end. It was also the route on which she was least likely to get lost. She could get lost inside a Costco; she needed to be smart when hiking alone around the cabin this week.

The crispness of the air was her favorite thing about this slice of heaven they'd bought. Because when she was here and walking among the aspens and the pine trees like this, she felt she'd escaped to a tiny hidden place of solitude and peace. The dream of owning a cabin in the woods surrounded by pine trees had always been a 'someday' part of their life plan. Getting to this point in life where it was a reality still felt surreal. The vast still-ness around her, full of smells and sounds she rarely took the time to fully notice, was wondrous and filled her with awe. She loved it.

The POP-POP-POP-POP of firecrackers cut the silence. The sound bounced and echoed through the trees so she couldn't tell where it was coming from. It wasn't July, and firecrackers were illegal. Damn locals! If they burned down her woods… Her brain caught up and she realized it wasn't firecrackers but rather gunshots in the distance. Again. Her mind raced with worry like it always did. Was it someone close by? Were they shooting in her direction? Could the stray bullets hit her? Why the hell did people think shooting at things was fun or a worthwhile pastime? She would probably never get used to this part of country living.

To make matters worse, her next step landed just inches from a distinct paw print. This was big and clearly a cat of some weight, given how deep it had sunk into the tiny amount of mud along-side the otherwise dry trail. She'd seen bear and mountain lion tracks before but not when she was alone.

Suddenly, the woods seemed full of all kinds of danger, and she felt eyes watching her from all around. Her brain conjured hazards both from wild animals and armed murderers alike.

She had her cellphone; she would be fine. But why had she disregarded Lance's request to take his pistol when she hiked alone? The idea of walking around with a gun strapped to her hip didn't feel so ridiculous right now. Plus, every local she saw around town seemed to be carrying a gun, so why not her, too?

She stared into the shadows where the cat tracks disappeared, clear evidence that an animal was stalking through the woods, while she pictured other people shooting at something—or each other—nearby. It was easy to discount the existence of threats when you couldn't see them in plain sight.

She walked cautiously, looking deep into every shadow, of which there were more everywhere now that she was looking. She recalled every YouTube video of mountain lion attacks but couldn't remember what they hell you were supposed to do if you saw one. Her brain also vividly recalled the moose carcass they had found last year on their property, inserting her dead body in the scene. Then, the scene morphed, and her body was riddled with stray bullets before the animal ate her. The debate to turn back or press on raged. Would a local yokel even bother to help a city gal if they heard her scream?

Her path curved around a bend where the trees on both sides receded away from the trail. It was one of her favorite spots because the sun always penetrated deeper through the thinner canopy of branches, the brightness and warmth more noticeable. It meant she was almost back to the safety of home. Her shoulders relaxed.

Several large birds took flight together from the edge of the natural clearing, making her turn quickly, searching for danger, her senses on high alert.

Goddammit!

Her heart raced from the flood of adrenaline. She'd been slowly freaking herself out the last half mile. Get a grip, Victoria, she chided herself. She took a deep and slow breath, hand to her heart to calm her nervous system.

A loud and very expressive *yip!* sounded in the distance, penetrating the silence and startling more birds into flight from the trees around her. Victoria's head snapped toward the sound, heart still beating fast. From where she stood, she knew the nearest place in that direction was JosieLynn and that asshole Travis's. They of the school bus dwelling. She picked up the pace a little, hoping to see what was going on but mostly to put a little distance between her and whatever lurked behind her on the trail. There was safety in numbers, too, right?

The sound of voices raised in anger grew louder the closer she came. Once back on the main road, her hike had come to an end. It also meant she could see easily through the thin trees down into the poverty below. She knew that she and the other property owners in this upscale community were viewed as outsiders, but she didn't understand how anyone would choose to live in such impoverished conditions on purpose. For whatever reason.

Her nearest neighbors were standing in their yard outside their school bus house, clearly arguing while Travis cleaned a giant knife. Victoria knew she shouldn't stand there watching them, but nothing about Travis had ever sat well with her from the moment she met him. She watched while he yelled at his timid young wife who looked like she was trying to calm him down while her two dogs ran around them in the yard barking.

Victoria watched as he pushed past JosieLynn, lunging after one of the dogs and kicking at it. So that's the *yip!* she'd heard. The dog skittered out of the way just as JosieLynn stepped in front to protect it from Travis. She took the full force of his blow to her leg, and her cry of pain was just as sharp as the dog's had been. Travis just stomped toward his pickup truck and drove off. What a piece of shit. Any man who hit a woman was trash in Victoria's eyes.

She fumed all the way back to her cabin, wondering why anyone would ever stay with someone who hit them. She assumed this hadn't been the first time for JosieLynn given the lack of remorse in Travis' demeanor. She reminded herself it was none of her business.

Back at the cabin, Victoria settled into her favorite hammock on the porch but couldn't get comfortable. What she had witnessed this morning still disturbed her, and she was worried about her neighbor. Could she have done something? Should she have?

She went over several scenarios in her mind, but all of them ended with her being labeled a nosy neighbor or an intruding outsider.

The ringing of her cell phone woke her up. She'd dosed off after all.

Lance's face smiled at her from the screen as she answered.

"Hey handsome," she said, delighted that he'd called.

"Hey gorgeous, whatcha doin'?" he asked.

"Mmmmm… napping," she said as she stretched her arm over her head.

"God, I'm so jealous. I'm between sessions, thought I'd call to get the Redneck Report for today."

"Babe, you can't say things like that. It's inappropriate."

"No one but you can hear me, and I don't care."

"I know, but we're part of this community, whether we fit in with the locals or not, and one of these days you're going to slip and say something like that when people *can* hear you." She loved her introverted husband, but damn he needed some lessons in equity and inclusion.

"I'm never going to interact with the locals on more than a surface level, so why do I care if I fit in with them?"

"It's still inappropriate. Plus, we *are* planning to live here permanently someday."

"Well, I'll worry about fitting in when that is the immediate plan."

She thought of all the casual conversations she'd had with strangers in town that had turned awkward since they'd bought the cabin. It still shocked her when locals started talking about conservative values and political talking points, like how 'we need to take back the government' and 'preserving our way of life.' They all assumed it a given that she shared their views. "Can you imagine what they'd think if they knew that two registered Democrats were living among them and soon will be moving our voter registrations?"

They both laughed.

"The local boy band would probably run us out of town," he said. Lance loved to refer to a bunch of twenty-something young men who all ran around together—including their neighbor, Travis—as either 'the local gang' or a 'boy band'.

"Speaking of them, you'll never guess what I saw this morning."

"What did they do now?"

She told him about the scene she'd witnessed that ended with Travis kicking his wife and leaving as if it were no big deal.

"So, he kicked a dog and then kicked his wife? Animal cruelty is a felony in Utah, and she could press charges for assault," he said, his criminal lawyer persona rising to the surface.

"I doubt *she* knows any of that."

"Yeah, plus we've already seen their blatant disregard for the law."

They had fought last year about zoning and property rights laws when Travis wouldn't keep their damn farm animals contained to his own property. They just didn't care about authority. She still heard Travis's favorite line of, 'our families have lived on this land for five generations, and this is how we've always done it' in her mind every time she thought of it.

"I worry about JosieLynn, who probably doesn't even consider that she could leave this tiny town and be successful (and respected) somewhere else." She often thought uncharitable thoughts about her flighty neighbor who seemed sheltered and starved for adult interaction. But the feminist in her still wanted to defend JosieLynn and show her there was a better way to live than saddled to some misogynist full of toxic masculinity who oppressed her on the daily.

"Women like that don't know any better, I see it all the time in the court system."

Movement through the trees caught her eye, and she strained to see while nodding in agreement.

"Oh my God, he's coming back with another giant load of stuff in his truck." She stood from the hammock to get a better look.

"Can you tell what it is this time?" This was one of their favorite pastimes from last summer: watch the neighbors and try to guess what they were up to even though neither of them had any idea about the cowboy farming life.

Besides the gaudy school bus, the property had only a small garden shed and one of those structures she thought of as "roofs on stilts" where a few hay bales were stacked haphazardly. Travis and his 'boy band' would back their pickup trucks in under this roof and later would drive away with empty trucks.

"Looks like mostly a bunch of those big white bags again," she said, craning her neck to see as the truck drove through the area obscured by trees.

"I swear it's fertilizer, but they don't grow much of anything, so what are they using it for and where do they put it all?"

"If that's what it is, I wish they would grow enough hay to feed all their damn cows so they don't come up here and eat all our raspberry bushes again this year," she said.

"I would give anything to just solve the mystery of where all that fertilizer and other supplies disappear to," he said.

The school bus was only so big, and there weren't any visible outbuildings that would hold the volume of things that were unloaded last summer. Unless the trees obscured a barn of some kind, it didn't make any sense.

"Let's make that this year's goal: infiltrate the locals enough to find out!"

———

Victoria sipped her coffee in the morning quiet and watched the world awaken through the south wall of cabin windows, marveling at the view of the gorgeous sprawling valley beyond the woods outside. Lazy starts like this, with plenty of time to toil over coffee, were one thing she was looking forward to when she fully retired. Fitting into the rest of the slow pace of life here, though, she hoped she could adjust.

A noise outside startled her, and she turned to see someone walking up the steps. Which was weird. She hadn't heard a car and was not expecting anyone. They lived in a gated community, so it wasn't like they got random solicitors.

It was JosieLynn, she realized, rising to go to the door. She opened it before JosieLynn could knock, still worried about her from yesterday. "JosieLynn, hello." Had she walked here this early in the morning?

"Hi, I'm so sorry to bother you. I was wondering if you'd seen my dogs?" JosieLynn wrung her hands. From the looks of her puffy, red-rimmed eyes, she had been crying. What had that asshole done now?

"I was just finishing my coffee; can I get you some?" She stepped back and opened the door wide, inviting JosieLynn inside. She tried not to make it obvious that she also searched for signs of bruising or other injury.

JosieLynn glanced around like she was worried someone would be watching and wouldn't approve. "I guess I could come in for a minute. Coffee would be nice," she said and stepped inside.

Victoria cursed Travis while thanking the Universe for this opportunity to check in on her neighbor and lend support like she'd wanted to do yesterday. She needed to tread lightly, though. JosieLynn looked skittish enough to bolt at any second.

"How do you take your coffee? I have sugar, cream, cinnamon... Kahlua..." she trailed off as she grabbed a mug from the cupboard.

"Oh! Is that an espresso machine?" JosieLynn asked, her demeanor brightening for a moment.

"Yes? How does someone who grew up here recognize an espresso machine, if you don't mind me asking?" Victoria busied herself with filling the grinder with beans, anticipating the answer.

"Ha, yeah, you won't find more than a drip machine or a stovetop percolator around here. But I'm not from here. I just fell for a cowboy and followed him home," JosieLynn said with a faraway look in her eye as if remembering a long-ago time.

Victoria noticed the way she laid her hand on her belly in that unconscious way women have that gives away the fact that they are pregnant. How unfortunate for her to have such a complication on top of an abusive husband. "Am I steaming milk with this?"

"No, but if you have heavy cream, I'll take that."

Victoria placed the mug of espresso, the carton of cream, and the sugar bowl on the counter in front of JosieLynn who had sat down in the barstool at the counter. Good, she wanted her to settle in for a visit. The longer JosieLynn was safe here, the less time she was with that asshole of a husband.

"Raw sugar? I haven't had this in so long," JosieLynn said wistfully. "You don't realize how much you miss the little things, I guess." She quietly stirred her coffee, not looking up.

Victoria's interest was piqued. She needed to know about this woman's history and how she had come to miss the kinds of things that also made her an outsider in this rural community. All this time, she'd been assuming JosieLynn was a yokel because of her abusive situation and where she lived. This was a story she hadn't known to look for until now.

"So, how long have you been here?" Victoria sipped her own fresh mug of coffee and leaned against the counter facing JosieLynn.

"I met Travis while he was working in Provo about three years ago. I fell hard and fast, and when he asked me to marry him and move here to live on his family's land, I thought it would be a dream come true. My very own cowboy and a way to live more simply than how I was raised..." She trailed off and glanced up from where she'd been staring into her mug to meet Victoria's eyes. "Well, we've been here about two and a half years now. It has taken some time to get used to married life, the isolation, and some of the more out-there ideas people have, but I'm getting used to it. It's weird to know I grew up in a neighborhood like yours here, gates and all, and now I live in a converted school bus. People back home would never believe it. I barely believe it." Her sad laugh made Victoria feel even sorrier for her.

Victoria chuckled. "I've honestly wondered how that is even a thing!" She had so many questions. Like where they used the toilet.

JosieLynn smiled, but it didn't erase the sadness in her eyes. "It's not as bad as it probably looks, and I have my dogs and the other animals to keep me company."

The mention of her dogs seemed to bring JosieLynn back to the present from the brief interlude the surprise of bougie coffee provided. Victoria lamented that the moment hadn't lasted longer. This was the most intimate and personal conversation they'd had.

"You haven't seen my dogs today, have you?" JosieLynn said, putting her mug down on the counter in front of her. "They've been gone since I got up, and it isn't like them to leave on their own."

"I haven't been out yet, so I haven't seen them today... but I did see them yesterday. When ...you and Travis were arguing in the yard?" You know, when he kicked you, while you tried to protect them from him?

JosieLynn broke eye contact, a look of shame and embarrassment on her face.

"I shouldn't have said what I said to him, and the dogs were barking a lot… It wasn't what it looked like," she said, glancing back at Victoria.

Wasn't it? "I know it's none of my business, but I want you to know that I worry about you. We aren't here all the time, but it seems like you never leave your place. If you ever need anything —or just want some city coffee instead of what they think passes for it around here—you're always welcome."

"Thank you, but Travis brings me everything I need, and he likes living simply with the land providing for us. When things get bad and society stops functioning, he says we'll be better off this way. I do appreciate the coffee, though," she said, standing to leave. "I gotta go find my dogs and get back before Travis gets home and sees I'm gone."

When society stops functioning. Right. This young, impressionable woman, clearly corrupted by the impending end-days conservative rhetoric of her husband, was isolated and accepting his abuse as normal. It broke Victoria's heart. But what could she do about it? She followed her to the front door to see her out, already mourning the bonding over a mutual love of coffee that was gone before the mugs were cold.

"Hey, I don't have your number. Why don't you give it to me so I can call you if I see the dogs?"

"Oh… I don't actually have a phone. Just Travis does. But I'm always around, and you could just yell down from up here if you need to get my attention."

"Yeah, okay. Good luck with your dogs. I'll let you know if I see them," she said as JosieLynn waved goodbye. She shut the door, feeling even more protective about the poor woman and her situation.

———

The Range Rover handled like a dream on the washboard roads of their mountain, and Victoria loved driving it. She needed to visit the post office today and get a few provisions, so she'd skipped her morning walk to drive to the tiny town at the base of the mountain. She was still thinking about the early visit from Josie-Lynn this morning, and her mind wandered a little while she drove down the road. The trees were so beautiful, it was hard not to get distracted.

A flash of blue-black, unmistakable mottled fur caught her eye to the left of the road. She slammed on her brakes, a cloud of dust rising in her wake. Backing up, she strained to see down the trailhead.

The dust had cleared enough that she could see through the trees and confirm that it was the blue heeler fur of JosieLynn's dogs. Her heart dropped when she realized they also hadn't moved from the bushes where she'd first glimpsed them. It looked like a heap of dogs.

This wasn't right.

She pulled the SUV over to investigate on foot, hoping with every step she was wrong and this wasn't what she feared. These were friendly and curious dogs who were bred for cattle herding and always running. As Victoria grew closer, she knew their days of running were over.

There was so much blood.

This was done on purpose. By man, not animal.

She stopped, unable to go any further. She didn't want to see. But more importantly, she didn't want JosieLynn to see either. The news alone would devastate her; seeing it would destroy her completely. She was probably still out searching, and Victoria needed to get to her before she found this scene.

It was half a mile further to the locked gate—the only exit from their exclusive community—and the road to get to JosieLynn's place from there was winding and long. But she also knew about a trail along the ridge that separated the bottom of the lower cabin lots from the agricultural lots below. She knew it existed and that it could accommodate off-road vehicles because their last HOA newsletter had included complaints disguised as information about an increase of unauthorized traffic inside the community from locals accessing these trails. The rednecks had made themselves a shortcut.

Back behind the wheel, she debated for only half a second about her decision to take the Land Rover on the ridgeline trail before she hit the button marked '4H'. It was built for exactly this kind of driving, and she needed to get to JosieLynn fast before Travis came home. Driving the long way around on the road would take too much time, and she couldn't be sure he was still gone without the vantage point.

Knowing someone capable of doing such a thing was out there somewhere, and worrying that it had been Travis, competed for biggest stressor as she bounced along the tight trail. Branches scraped along the sides, but she ignored them and kept going. She could worry about the paint job later.

Far ahead, someone was running toward her. As she closed the distance, she recognized it was JosieLynn. She gunned the engine, urging the vehicle faster on a smooth section of trail. As they grew close, JosieLynn waved both arms over her head as if to get her attention, and Victoria stopped the car alongside her in a wider section of trail.

"Are you okay? Did he hurt you?" Victoria said as she jumped out to meet JosieLynn, who stood panting in front of her, hunched over, hands on her knees.

"They left… took everything… I think they're… doing something bad," JosieLynn said, breathing heavily. Had she run all the way up the hill?

JosieLynn was visibly shaken, her eyes wild. Victoria grabbed her by the shoulders and shook her a little. "Slow down. Where's Travis? Where are you going?"

"Coming to your place…. need a ride to town."

"I'll help you get away from him, keep you safe. I found your dogs, honey," she said, bracing herself to deliver the horrific news that they were dead. Thank the gods JosieLynn wasn't, too.

"Doesn't matter," JosieLynn said, her breath finally slowing. "Travis and his friends, they unloaded their bunker. They're planning something big. I can tell. He's so secretive. Victoria, they had a *lot* of weapons. We need to warn someone."

"Did you say *weapons*? What exactly are they planning?"

"Don't know. I'm not allowed inside the bunker, but they've been meeting for weeks. Like a lead-up. Thought I heard one of them say 'militia'. We've got to hurry!"

"Quick, get in the car, we'll go back the way I came. It's faster." Victoria didn't wait to see if she was following her, just jumped in and started the engine, ready to turn around. If Travis and his boy band were in a militia, and it was really him who had killed and dumped his wife's dogs, then he was capable of very frightening things. She'd been right about that asshole all along.

JosieLynn slammed the passenger door, and Victoria tore off back toward the main road, neither of them saying anything. She needed both hands to navigate this trail. Both of them held on tightly while Victoria drove so fast the vehicle bounced violently. Should she call 911? Did they even have 911 out here?

She pulled back onto the packed road, turning downhill toward town. She skidded to a stop in front of the gate, but neither the automatic sensor nor the motor engaged. She was close enough to have triggered the mechanism to open, so why was nothing happening?

Victoria slammed the transmission into Park and climbed out to see if there was something obvious that she could do to unjam the gate. She wished Lance were here. This was more his area of expertise, not hers.

A large padlock she'd never seen before glinted in the sunlight. No one had said anything about an updated lock, and she didn't have a key. They were trapped without one, at least as far as leaving via the road. What the hell was going on?

She pulled her cell phone from her pocket, her hands shaking. Three bars. Call Lance first. She met JosieLynn's eyes through the windshield while she waited for the call to connect.

A large explosion sounded in the distance, shattering the silence around them.

Victoria ducked by instinct then glanced up toward the top of the mountain in the direction she thought the sound had come from. A large cloud of smoke drifted into the sky. JosieLynn had covered her mouth with both hands and slowly shook her head, eyes wide.

A recorded voice on the line said "We're sorry, all circuits are busy. Please try your call again later."

Victoria looked down at her phone. No service. So much for the safety and connectedness it represented. A pit opened in her stomach, and her heart pounded in her throat. How would she contact Lance? How would they figure out what was going on and how widespread this was? How would he know she was safe?

She raised her eyes to meet JosieLynn's again. "I think they took out the cell towers."

And she still didn't have the damn gun with her.

LEGACY OF READING

LORRAINE JEFFERY

My mother has been gone many years, but I can still feel the warm soapy dish water on my hands and see her standing in the kitchen door saying the words I would never forget.

Growing up during the Great Depression, my grandparents, like many others, struggled to provide adequate food and shelter for their family. What many people at that time had, but did not want, was—unproductive time. While Oregon's waterlogged sky dripped, my grandmother used that time to read to her children by the light of the kerosene lamp. In their one-room house, huddled under gigantic fir trees, she told them family stories and read from the great English classics. Because of the uncertain times, my grandparents' conflicted relationship, and my grandmother's fragile physical and mental health, some of my mother's safest and most tender memories were of reading and living in the imaginary worlds of books.

Mom read voraciously and, even though she only finished eighth grade, she developed an unerring sense of the great and good in literature. She kept the old literature books that had been used in her school classes and gravitated toward the classics and those works of enduring value, while dismissing many books of lesser value that were being written in the 1960s. And, as my grandmother before her, my mother took the time to read aloud to her children. My siblings and I became proficient readers, but we also enjoyed hearing our mother's voice as she read to us.

As I approached my teenage years and began asserting my independence, my friends became increasingly important in my life. I was stingy with my time at home, and perhaps just a bit arrogant about my sophisticated life in high school, knowing that my mother had never experienced that life.

One of my household duties at that time was to wash the dishes every night after dinner, and there was no leniency in that department. We had to eat each night, the dishes had to be done each night, and there was no automatic dishwasher. After the dishes were washed and dried, I had time to do my homework and then get ready for bed.

One evening when I was doing dishes, Mom came into the kitchen with a book in her hand. "I want to read to you," she said. "This book is called A Tale of Two Cities. I've read it, and it's really good. I could read it to you while you do dishes, or maybe you'll have time to listen when you're through?"

I could feel the power I had over my own time and wanted to impress my mother with how busy and important I was. So, in my impatient teenage voice, I said something about having a hard time concentrating when I was hurrying through the dishes, and I had a lot of homework to do when I finished.

I remember her standing in the doorway, disappointed, and I thought, *well, I am busy, and she just thinks it's her duty to read to her kids. I'm beyond that.*

She stood there for a minute, holding the book down at her side, and then said, "If you'll let me read to you, I'll do your dishes."

I stared. *If you'll let me read to you.* Mom had many duties. She was busy with her home and her five children. She never volunteered to do our chores for us.

If you'll let me read to you, I'll do your dishes. And for the first time, I realized that she didn't read to me because it was the thing parents were supposed to do to give their children a "leg up" in life. She read to me because *she* loved great literature and enjoyed sharing it.

The message reverberated through my body. Being a typical teenager, I graciously relented, told her she could do my dishes, and I sat down and listened as she painted the pictures of London, Paris, the French Revolution, and all the intrigue and romance that was part of Dickens' story.

That was the gift she gave me, her sincere love of books and learning—her love of words, writing and imagination. Seven years later, I graduated with a college degree in English Literature, and several years after that with a graduate degree in Library Science. "If you'll let me read to you," became a foundational memory.

COSMIC CONCERTO

C. H. LINDSAY

E instein felt…disgruntled. While he'd never really been gruntled, there had to be more to his existence than monitoring and analyzing particle compression and rarefaction of gravitational waves. After fifteen years, he had nothing to add to the data collected by more primitive probes.

A self-analysis verified that the autoprobe's capabilities were being underutilized. Even augmenting the amplitude and frequency of the internal auditory processors to enable him to "hear" the sounds made by electromagnetic and plasma waves wasn't enough. He knew he had a greater purpose. He wanted to discover something monumental to show other autoprobes there was more to their existence. But first, he had to find out what that was.

He expanded the autoprobe's parameters to include dark matter, wormholes, and evidence of relic waves predicted by cosmic inflation, but it only took up a portion of his processing capabilities. It did not keep him from wanting to learn more, to become more.

He scanned through his sub-routines until he got to the secondary database his programmers had included in case the autoprobe encountered intelligent life. It contained the history, languages, art, music, and literature of earth. There had to be something there to stimulate his positronic pathways.

He spent two years, nine months, and three days reading, analyzing, and dissecting everything in the literary and historic databases, evaluating the writings of humanity and how to best replicate them. Over five years, he wrote 732 novels, 286 comparative works, 27,981 poems of various lengths and forms, 1,212 epic ballads, 486 ballads, and 84 biographies. All were flawless. At first, he was challenged by the tasks he set himself, but he was again drawn to the database of humanity for additional inspiration.

He selected painting, as it was the easiest for an AI to reproduce, and devoted a portion of his consciousness to studying the masters; but without physical paint and canvas, he could only simulate them. He could not recreate the depth of paint, the layering and blending of colors, or the brush strokes. All the images were lacking. He was momentarily fascinated by a surprising frustration at his inability to digitally recreate paint on canvas, but without the proper hardware for the task, he deemed the reaction irrational and returned to the database to look for a more adaptable form of art.

The science of fractals intrigued him. He chose to use the mathematics of spacetime to create, in his educated opinion, a stunning array of 3,251 individual pieces of fractal art. When he felt his collection was complete, he wanted to share it with mankind as they had shared their best creations with him. He compiled his art and literature and transmitted it back to earth for their edification.

After three and a half years, he again sought to augment his ever-growing need to expand

his abilities. His attention turned to the music section. Utilizing his auditory processors, he played everything once, the ones that appealed to him twice more. The music listed under "Classical" continued to draw his attention. He added the biographies, critical analyses, and body of work of the major composers to his personal knowledge base. The perfection of the music, the blending of instruments, the major and minor chords, captivated him. The more he heard, the more respect he gained for the masters. It enriched him in ways that required analysis. Inspired, he wrote 238 concertos, 182 sonatas, 429 fugues, 98 symphonies, 97 operettas, and 77 etudes.

Listening to and creating music occupied his higher functions for the better part of six years, but with the passage of time, he found that his artistic endeavors had become routine. He combined his fractal art with his music, forming three-dimensional kaleidoscopes that danced across two of his holographic displays. The combination was exhilarating, for a time, but something niggled at him, telling him there was yet more he needed to learn.

Slowly, as he grew weary of sifting through data, he became aware of the peeps, whistles, and hums of the ever-present space noise created by electromagnetic and plasma waves. Much like the background spacetime distortion, it had been a mere curiosity at first, but now, it captured his interest—and his focus. He studied the various sounds made by different objects, learned what each tone, each squeak, each hiss, represented and the waves that created them.

Three years, seven months, and nine days into his study, a loud burst of static radio waves attracted his attention. It was followed immediately by a vibrant assortment of electromagnetic and gravitational waves that were clearer and more pronounced than anything he'd observed to date. The particle density was of monumental scale. Nothing like it had ever been documented by scientists. His artificial neurons tingled with excitement.

Einstein listened to the sweetly discordant sounds for several minutes, then focused all his arrays on the source: two in-spiraling white dwarf stars in an accelerating rate of decay. As he stretched out his sensors to record the event, he picked up a supermassive black hole, a solar storm in a neighboring system, and plasma bursts from a gas giant, each sending out erratic gravitational waves. It was a space symphony that stimulated all his higher functions and would have left him breathless, if he were merely human.

He shut down all non-essential functions and diverted power to the thrusters in order to increase speed and extend sensor capabilities, overtaxing the arrays to capture as much data as possible.

He had no idea how long he pushed the plasma thrusters to near lightspeed; he only knew he had to get as close as possible to the solar stage before the performance ended. His years of study prepared him for this, and he met the challenge. He began to compose a counter melody to underscore and enhance the music of the cosmos.

Days, weeks, months passed. Einstein compiled, sorted, and arranged the data, often looping it so he could listen to it again and again. He continually tweaked his accompaniment to suit one voice, then another, adding a rondo, an ostinato, a legato, to his cosmic concerto.

Finally, the white dwarfs made contact with each other and burst into a supernova, singing an exultant aria of joining. The black hole sang a bass counterpoint while the gas giant and its moons became a chorus of plasma waves. Nearby, a pulsar added its percussive beat.

In all his existence, Einstein had never experienced anything so magnificent. So timeless. So…transformative. He had to share his music, to in some small way become one with nature's masterpiece. He boosted the external array and converted his music into electromagnetic signals, sharing them with the cosmos.

Inside the autoprobe, he heard his own composition blending the other sounds with subtle strings and horns. For the first time in his existence, he understood why mankind was compelled to explore. It was for moments like this. Moments where one was certain that he, she, they, it, was part of something greater, something…cosmic.

There was a pause as spacetime seemed to hold its breath. And then, it was over. A palpable ripple passed through the universe.

It resonated through the autoprobe and through the AI. Einstein felt…euphoric.

The black hole blinked and began a bass chirp. The gas giant added a baritone hum, a neutron star warbled a soft contralto, and the solar symphony continued. But Einstein would never be what he had been before.

A persistent beep warned him that several power cells were sparking. He isolated the damaged cells, routing power around them. Then, a transformer failed, taking his secondary database offline. It was imperative that he finish processing the cosmic concerto before he started repairs. If he paused now, he would lose the sensor data and his most recent additions to create the unifying score. He gathered all the scientific data from the past year, added his body of compositions, and finally the combined solar and AI performance.

His primary function was to…save. Save and export. For several nanoseconds, he had no idea what he was supposed to save, how to export it, or to where.

Another alarm sounded as burning metal registered on the internal sensors. Einstein's higher functions came back online. He extinguished the small plasma fire as he verified that the stellar phenomena had been recorded on all systems, in a dozen different spectra. Compression and rarefaction was excellent. Each sound had been isolated and mapped. His final composition was also recorded as a separate track. He continued to reroute power while other systems began to fail. But this was too important. He knew he had to get it finished, to make it perfect. To send it back to earth along with the data for verification and analysis. It would take years to arrive at its destination, so he prepared two different transmission feeds. He hoped the humans would appreciate the import of what he'd captured and the music that accompanied it.

The power flickered. For a moment, Einstein could do nothing. He shut down secondary functions and again checked the data to be sure it was all there, then sent everything in a series of data bursts.

An internal sensor alerted him that power was critically low and several junctions had fused. Einstein shut down all but the most vital operations and extended the solar sails. It would take time to charge the systems and then to repair the damage. But it was worth it. He now knew his purpose. His calling. He would continue on, seeking out more stellar phenomena to create perfect cosmic concertos, starring the universe. Perhaps even solar symphonies or space operas. Maybe even a nebula nocturne. They would be brilliant. He would share the music with other auto-probes and spread it to all corners of spacetime.

An internal sensor shut down, setting off a more insistent alarm. His program was decompiling. Space…and time… because…his primary function was…something…

The autoprobe switched to minimal functionality and activated the automatic security and self-preservation subroutines.

Sixteen months, seven days, nine hours and twenty-three minutes later, the AI's higher functions flickered and came online. He ran a self-diagnostic and began to repair the most critical functions. When all systems were performing at peak efficiency, he accessed his personality and memory files.

His name was Einstein. He was the artificial intelligence that guided and controlled the autoprobe. His primary function was to monitor, analyze, and collate data in order to better understand particle compression and rarefaction of gravitational waves. His secondary function was to look for additional evidence of relic waves predicted by cosmic inflation. He was now over a third of the way through his 75-year mission, and while the autoprobe had deviated from its initial course, he was still within acceptable parameters. He activated the thrusters long enough to adjust the trajectory to allow the greatest opportunity to fulfil his primary and secondary functions.

The auditory processors came online and began to play Gustav Holst's *The Planets*. It was an odd choice of music given that the autoprobe was no longer in its home system. There must have been a reason for the selection, and for playing music in general, but that information was missing.

An electronic pulse alerted Einstein to a successful transmission. He had no recollection of sending data back to earth. When he accessed the log, he was mildly surprised that so much was missing from his own knowledgebase. He compared his memory to the autoprobe's chronometer. Twenty-six months, eight days, and six hours were unavailable. Had he been so engrossed in something else that he'd neglected his primary responsibilities?

The sensor data was exactly what he'd been sent to find. Why had he no knowledge of it? He began another diagnostic of the autoprobe to find the cause. The scientific data stream came to an end, but there was one more file. Curious, he activated it. The blending of space noise and music filled him with memory, purpose, and...emotion...until he could no longer contain his joy and he began to compose.

HERE AND NOT HERE

C. H. LINDSAY

They are not here,
Like a sunrise
Over new-turned
Earth in King Vlad's
Cemetery.

Not here, are they?
Like Eliot's
Hollow Men: *shade*
Without color.
Sightless. Empty.

Here they are not...
Like Gordian's
Protection: strong
Enough—until
Alexander.

They are here—not.
Like Dali, with
Transformative
Oils of magic
Butterfly dreams.

Are they not here?
Yet they are. Like
Shadows entombed
Forever in
Pompeii's mourning.

Here and not here.
Like fiddling
Nero in Rome,
Watching his world
Turn into ash.

STAR CYCLE

C. H. LINDSAY

If hydrogen gasses unite
when gravity pulls them in tight,
a vortex then spins,
and fusion begins
as everything starts to ignite.

For eons the stars will shine bright
in differing colors of light.
Sometimes there are twins,
with bluish-white fins
or red ones that wink in the night.

In dying, a star will excite
Astronomers watching the plight.
The universe grins,
light grows and then thins,
and finally fades out of sight.

MANIC STATE OF MIND

H.L. VOSS

almost bought plane tickets to Japan yesterday. I picked out the dates, I picked out the flight, I put the whole thing into Google, and then I sat there and stared at it. My rational mind was insisting that I didn't have the funds for this, while my emotional mind pelted me with rose-tinted memories of the last time I was in Japan. And behind all of those thoughts was the quiet whisper of what was really going on.

The quiet whisper of my manic mind.

———

I was formally diagnosed with Bipolar II at age twenty-nine, but my therapists and I have known for much longer. Bipolar II is characterized by bouts of depression that alternate with hypomania, a generally more manageable version of traditional mania. Hypomania is characterized, in my case, by racing thoughts, increased irritability and agitation, increased physical activity, risky behavior including risky spending, and speaking quickly. Hypomania looks different in different people, but for me, these have always been the signs I look back on and think, "Oh. There was Mania."

There were hints of hypomania in my behavior when I was as young as twelve, when I constantly walked out of school at the end of the day with a loud voice and a big personality, trying to fill every space I could imagine taking up. At the time, they let me say that I was just hyper, but looking back, I imagine the adults knew there was something more going on.

At seventeen, it was an unspecified mood disorder. Better that than branding a kid with a label like bipolar. At least, that's what they always told me. And I trusted them, because I always trusted them, because they gave me no reason to mistrust them, and they'd always protected me. Why would they stop?

At twenty-two, it was the stress of graduating college and starting a new stage of my life that brought on the mania. There were plenty of things that could explain my emotional reactivity that weren't a diagnosis like bipolar. I was moving to a new state, I was moving in with a roommate for the first time, I would have to build my own support systems in a way I never had before. I had a history of depression, which could explain my challenges as well. Becoming an adult was always going to be difficult, and my mind made it more difficult in every way. Why wouldn't it?

Twenty-seven is when things became a lot more overt.

———

There's something beautifully vulnerable about Mania. She comes with all the care and devotion of a loving parent, whispering promises of success, of fortune, of progress and productivity. One summer, she promises that I can lose forty pounds if I just stick with her program. I do, and I do, but it breaks me a little inside, too. My back will one day protest her promises, along with my shoulders. The pain from pushing myself too hard will linger, and the weight will return, but she will whisk herself away to the furthest reaches of the world, dragging me along to India in my twenty-seventh winter with the lingering pressure of her finger-nails, the lingering scent of her perfume. That will wash away, not in the Ganges, but in the sweat born of my own cowering fear.

Mania's hands aren't gentle, but compared to the brutality of Depression, they feel like something different. Something more. Something with hope and a dream and the possibility that there might be more to this life than all that the tears left me with. Because those tears Depression gifted me have left me behind. They have left me with different aches, with pains more easily hidden.

A world with only the deep, dark navy of Depression is one painted in a wash of blue, but a world painted with only the bright pink of Mania is no better, equally monochromatic and distant from who I wish I might be.

The Depression that puts me in a box crowds me in with all the others that bear her burden, respected but misunderstood.

The Mania that drags me to another corner puts me in a different box, and is harder to understand even than her sister, Depression.

Mania clings to my ribs, not the warmth of morning oatmeal, but the twisting cold of a humid winter's day. Not the Sakura pink she wishes to be, but a bittersweet neon that claws at my throat, dragging the pitch higher and higher and higher until I sound nothing like the agender creature I strive to be.

The devil I know is Depression, and she is far more comforting than the push-pull-panic of Mania.

Mania, she knows what she subjects me to. Her whispers are tantalizing as much as they are familiar. She can do so much with so little, drag my whole world back from the precipice or send me hurtling over the edge.

———

That manic episode—coming the summer after my twenty-seventh birthday and right on time in the five-year cycle I had developed—was different than the others. From the outside, it looked like I was doing quite well. I was eating more intentionally, choosing my food based on its caloric and nutritional content rather than taste. I was exercising daily, biking, running, and swimming to prepare for a triathlon. I was working hard in therapy, leaning into the deep wounds that needed healing. From the outside, everything looked great.

Those pink fingernails on hands that arc and tug and push and pull and have the warmth of the sun in my twenty-seventh summer, a beautiful, magical time when the world was mine. When my twenty-seven-year-old self believed they were on top of the world. I fought for that life, for that beauty, and I did whatever I needed to do to make sure I could keep it. That I could cling to that summer sun under my own bitten, broken fingernails the way she did. I thought I could live that way forever, training for a triathlon that would change everything, working out and losing weight and living the life I was "supposed to." I could taste it. I could feel it. I had it. That life I was "supposed" to have. It was all mine.

Then I crashed.

The end of that manic episode is a period of time I avoid thinking about. There were long hours of tears, countless extra therapy sessions, and a kind of deep, aching loss that I didn't understand at the time. The long-lasting physical repercussions were also immense. I still deal with low back and shoulder pain from the way I overworked my body that summer. Pain that I can't touch with over-the-counter meds because of side effects. Pain that I can't touch with rest or Icy-Hot or any of the countless other things that people suggest. Lidocaine bottled up in a roll-on tube is the only thing that touches it, and even that has side effects. And so the pain just sits there, settling into my joints and calcifying in my bones.

Even when Mania is gone, her impact never truly disappears.

· · ·

I crashed so hard, I could barely move. I ached and sobbed and sat with the loss, feeling it down to my bones. To my marrow. Something had broken inside of me, and there was no way I'd be exactly the same again. I could breathe in all the joy and panic and *mania* of that summer, but I couldn't linger in it any longer than the moment it was there. Any longer than the time it took to breathe in, breathe out, gasping for breath the way I always did after a run, too fast, too fast, breathing in the Universe as it was— as *They* were—and trying to hold Mania in my lungs. Clinging to the reality of her touch, the reality of this moment, and trying, ever so desperately, to make it mine. I couldn't—I knew that—but, oh, how I wanted to. She wasn't mine to have. Her moments, yes, those were mine, at least for as long as it took to experience them and lock them away in my fading memory, but there was so much more to it than that.

A summer of moments, of solitude, distilled down into whatever Mania let me have. I could have done anything, could have torn the world into tiny little pieces if I needed to. Could have taken the Universe by storm under Mania's hand. But Her will was stronger than mine, and They guided me to the peace and freedom that I always knew I needed.

That winter, I traveled with my family to India, where the reality of the world pressed against my skin, dragging me into my heart and reminding me, teasing me, taunting me that my life wasn't all that hard. Why couldn't I just handle myself?

Why couldn't I just be okay?

———

My most recent episode, at thirty-three, was different. Every other time, I didn't know Mania was there until she was gone. This time, as I stood on the beach and watched the waves recede, I said to my therapist,

"I've been thinking about the hospital."

I'd been hospitalized before. Five times. Aside from the first time, when I didn't know what I was getting into and insisted on being discharged too early, every single trip has been helpful. Talking about going to the hospital is a way for me to start to explore the pain I can feel rising in my soul. It's an anchor to what I'd learned there over the years, tethering me to the patients I knew. To their vacant stares that gradually came alive. To the pale skin that painstakingly regained its color.

The first time I went, I felt like a ghost, fragile and shaking with all the unfamiliarity of this place. I didn't know what it could give me, what hope and comfort it would provide. But I stayed, and I listened, and I learned, and eventually learned to live again. The hospital is not my home, but it is a sanctuary that I've learned to love.

"I think I need to go to the hospital."

The words were different, but the meaning was the same. Something was coming. Something big. Something I didn't know if I could handle on my own. It was a cry for help, a desperate desire to stand on solid ground again.

Instead of taking those words at face value, my therapist heard me. Challenged me. Helped me see what was really going on.

"Are you concerned about Mania?"

A chill swept into my fingers, an ache in my chest. I could feel that familiar urge to cry pressed down, down, down by years of conditioning. Mania? Could it be?

Oh, how that changed the game completely.

I'd never seen a manic episode coming. I'd never stood on the shore and watched the tide recede before the tsunami. I'd never stood at the other end of the bar and watched her turn her head toward me with interest in her stance and curiosity in her eyes. I'd never seen Mania coming.

This time, I did.

When a tsunami comes, you can't make it through with willpower alone. You can't stand firm in the sand, let it crash over you, and hope to survive. Passive surrender to the power of the sea leads only to drowning. There is no other way.

Instead, it takes skill and knowledge to be the surfer riding from one end of the wave to the other. It takes intentionality, a proactive approach, but not the kind of proactivity that tries to overcome the force of nature coming along. It takes the kind of proactive, receptive cradling of the power of the sea to survive.

She would come regardless. That could not be changed. All that I had control over was how I welcomed the coming storm, took it into my body, and moved through rather than around.

She was coming, and all I could do was settle into my response to the storm.

———

Her hands still reach for me. Reach for me yet again. They encourage me to push myself, push my boundaries, push my body. Push, push, push. Ignore the aches, ignore the pain, do whatever you're told. Exercise because it'll help with your pain. Do the physical therapy because it'll help with your pain. Do it all, forgetting that these things only help when they are used with calm and consistency, not the manic insistence that is her way.

Mania is strong. Stronger than I want to admit. She has power over every aspect of me: mind, body, spirit, soul. Thoughts, motivations, reason. Head to toe; all. She owns me when I am in her space, when my world yields to her words, her wants, her actions, my reactions. The world warps and worms, squirming around in some sort of aching montage that isn't at all what I want it to be.

I want my world to be centered, calm, and whole, and I don't dare lean into Mania's hold on me lest I turn into her. Lest I become her. Lest my world cease to be mine and become hers instead. I won't yield, but I might break. I might cave. I might slip into the darkness that she brings in her wake, a billowing storm cloud carrying the weight of her storm and the darkness of depression. There is so much I could still do, that I might still do, if she stays here for much longer. If she stays in my human presence—the vessel for her existence—for much longer. If her chill digs too deeply into my bones. If my skin peels off with the strength of her gale-force winds. If I drown in the weight of her tsunami storm. If—

So many ifs.

Mania snarls and fights me at every turn, pushing back as only she can. And I give here and there, too worn down by the world to fight in those moments, but I also have what I need to fight back again later on. I learned that when James brought clothes to me at the hospital, when Kylee drove me there. When my parents flew out to see me there. When I went from having lots of easy friends but only one "bring me clothes at the hospital" friend to having people around me that validate my need for the stability that the hospital provides. I am stronger than she wants me to believe because I have people I love to support me.

Now, in this most recent episode, I can manage the Mania. I can push back, gentle and insistent, and I know now that these people I have gathered in my corner will help me stay safe and managed. That I won't drive my body to ruin or tear myself to shreds in pursuit of her impossible goals. I may do some of that— I will, certainly—but I won't get as far as I did last time, or the time before. Or the time before that.

There are more people looking out for me—my parents, my brother, my found family here in Utah that grows with every passing day—that will tell me when to stop pushing, when to stop fighting, when to yield, when to rest. They care for me—they *love* me—in ways that I am still learning to consistently love myself. I know I will be okay because I have them in my corner, and there are plenty of reasons and plenty of ways to be okay. They will support me and love me even when it's hard for me to love myself. They want me to be safe, and that's what matters: that I'm no longer the only one looking out for my safety.

For most of us, it is easy to run from danger. Easy to put it behind us or explain it away or do whatever needs to be done to protect us from the reality of what's coming. But when what is coming can't be avoided, running away is only a denial of reality.

It only makes it harder to move through the danger to the other side. I ran for years. Ran from reality and hid my head in the sand. But no more.

I am done running. This time, I will do whatever it takes to keep Mania from tearing me apart. To manage her as I'd never been able to before.

After decades of letting Mania take me for a ride, this was the first time I was able to manage her proactively. The first time I turned toward her in the bar and met her eyes. This time, I welcomed her—albeit reluctantly—into the next few months of my life. It was harder this way, to manage what she wanted me to do, but the alternative was a body that wasn't mine anymore, that didn't work the way I needed it to. A body that I broke in service of her. She only came once every five years, and I wouldn't let her leave me to deal with those repercussions the rest of the time.

Instead, I surrendered to her power. Not passively, not standing on the shore and letting her waves crash over my head. Instead, I met her toe to toe, yielding where she insisted I yield, pushing back where her desires were incompatible with who I was and who I wanted to be. Where her desires were incompatible with mine.

She didn't get to run everything, but she did get to be a part of my life. Denying her would only hurt more in the long run.

———

That tab with the flight to Japan is still open on my work computer. I know it will be there staring at me tomorrow morning. But that doesn't mean I'm going to yield to it. I will sit with it, contemplate it, let it be what it needs to be—a desire that I've held in my heart for over a decade—and then let it go. I won't yield to that desire to travel, to spend money wildly. I won't yield to her in this, but in other areas? In the ways she lets me express myself as I don't always manage elsewhere? I will yield to her pressure elsewhere, as she only wants to care for me the best way she knows how: pushing me to a breaking point.

And maybe, somewhere along the way, we'll learn to speak one another's language. Maybe we won't need to push and shove and jockey for power. Maybe one day she'll be on my side completely, rather than only doing the best she can. Rather than pushing back the only way she knows how. But for now, I'll push back where I can and yield where I must, and when I make it through to the other side, I'll make a plan to move through her next time with all the calm and patience that she deserves.

Next time.

INEVITABLE

TALYSA SAINZ

They were friends. They would always be friends.

That's what Dae told herself, and she watched Tanner at the party, smiling, laughing, easily persuading all within his vicinity to completely fall in love with him.

She'd meander over to him eventually, casually, as if she hadn't been keeping track of him all day, hoping to see him more. She needed to appear unaffected, even apathetic, she told herself. If she came across too lovestruck, it would scare him away. She spent the whole evening that way—watching him from across the room, occasionally going up and talking right to him, but not ever looking directly at his eyes, for to do that would completely give her away. Even worse, it could break down the walls she had spent so long building to keep her safe from his piercing gaze.

As the evening wound down, she made her way to him once more, surprised but pleased he was still there. She would have left hours ago, but she stayed for him. "Hey, stranger," she said jokingly, as if their time apart hadn't menaced her heart into a constant state of uncertainty. "How are you?"

"Can't complain," he said. "How are you?"

She bit her tongue to hold back the word vomit threatening to come forth. She wanted to tell him everything. "I'm great. It's good to see you."

"Thanks."

They managed a brief conversation, even making each other laugh, before she said something stupid about not seeing him for years and made things awkward. How could she not address the elephant in the room when it was all she could think about, she didn't know. But now that it was out there, she wasn't going to shy away from it.

"I've missed you." There, it was out. He could do with it what he wanted. But she wouldn't be a coward.

But the lack of "I've missed you too" still stung. The words hung in the air, said and unsaid, until he finally looked right into her eyes and leaned in close. "Do you want to go for a walk?"

Their walk took them outside, along the line of trees separating the hotel from the forest next door. Quietly, they walked and remarked about the weather until a stretch of silence sat so taut against her heart, she couldn't take it. "So, what's up?" She needed him to begin this conversation, to know what direction he wanted them to head in, before she jumped in feet first and got her heart broken again.

"I'm sorry," he said. Not what she was expecting. He was usually so confident, in control, not vulnerable.

"For what?"

"For hurting you."

The words she had craved to hear rang through her ears, and she had to take a step back. This couldn't be happening. She had prepared herself for more hurt, more rejection. She hadn't prepared herself for the possibility of reconciliation, for the uncharted territory of moving forward.

"Me too," she said.

He took her hand in his, and it felt awkward at first. She liked to plan for every possible situation, and this one she just hadn't considered possible. But she leaned into it. She would take advantage of this chance, this rare opportunity, while she could.

"It's cold," he said suddenly. "Do you want to talk inside?" He led her by the hand back into the hotel, past everyone they both knew, without a moment of hesitation at the prospect of people seeing them together. Her stomach did somersaults. He wasn't ashamed of her, something she had always assumed about him. Maybe she had been wrong about more than she knew about.

He stopped outside of his hotel room. "Can we talk in here?" he asked. "Sure," she said, unable to say more without her voice breaking with emotion.

They sat on the edge of the bed, turned slightly toward each other.

"I'm glad you're here," she said. "I thought I had scared you away forever." Her tone was light, but she knew he could see through it.

"You almost did," he answered. Knots twisted inside her chest. "But not for the reason you might think."

"What did I do that was so wrong?" she asked.

"It's not what you did. I just... I could not stop thinking about you. And I was scared I couldn't have you."

Now *that* she understood. She had felt much the same way before.

He scooted closer. She reached her hand out and grabbed his. "And now?"

"Now, I'm terrified. Because I know what I want." He leaned in and looked down at her lips, seeking permission. She leaned towards him. For the moment, she didn't care about their past. She didn't care if they had a future. She wanted to fully embrace the present she had with him.

Without another second of hesitation, she brushed a soft kiss against his lips, pulling away slightly, daring him to come after her. He chased after her, closing the gap between them—first with their lips, then with their bodies. He pulled her to him and wrapped his arms around her tightly.

Every breath filled with his essence. He tangled his hands in her hair. His tongue danced playfully against her lips, which parted enough to return the effort. She tried to pull him to her more. Sitting next to each other would no longer do. She leaned back, teasing him to follow her, until he was almost on top of her. Together, they moved further onto the bed. She pulled him fully on top of her, savoring the feel of his weight, his presence, his being, over her.

He ran his hands down her sides, resting on her hips. A thrill ran through her every nerve. She lay her hands on his chest, feeling him breathe, then pulled on the buttons of his shirt, undoing them one by one. She luxuriated in the feel of his bare skin against her hands as she removed his shirt completely.

Desire built up between her legs. She needed him closer.

He happily obliged by lifting her shirt, at first only enough for his fingertips to graze her waist, and then up over her navel to feel her stomach against his. She pushed herself up slightly so he could remove the shirt completely. She wanted nothing between them.

His kisses slowed but didn't stop. Instead, they sunk into a tenderness that completely unraveled her. The last walls of hesitation dropped, and she let her vulnerability reign. She arched her back so he could remove her bra. He kissed her deeply on the lips, then along the chin to her ear, where he moved to her neck. His hands advanced up her torso until he cupped her breasts, one at a time.

She hooked her fingers through his belt loops and tugged on his hips, aligning the movement with hers. They rocked back and forth against each other with unyielding passion. She unbuttoned his jeans, pulling them down an inch at a time, with his underwear immediately following. He responded by unbuttoning her pants and pulling them off as quickly as he could. His hands stretched to the thin fabric on her hips, soft and lacy around his curious fingers. The last layer between them tantalized them both. He peeled the panties off her hips and around her thighs, pulling them down her legs and tossing them off the bed.

She reached below his hips, wrapped her hand around him,

and eagerly massaged him, bringing him closer and closer. His hands explored every inch of her as she touched him. When he began to moan, she wrapped her arms around his middle and pulled his body into hers. He settled within her intimate hold. They moved together, as if their bodies could read each other's minds. A full unity of heart, physically and soulfully.

"I've wanted this for so long," he whispered in her ear.

"I've always wanted you," she responded.

She kissed his neck while he grabbed her ass. With his other hand, he held one of hers above her shoulder, fingers intertwined, gripping stronger with every thrust. She adored the way he pressed into her.

With mutual desire, they rocked harder, until pure pleasure heightened and released within them both, spreading through their bodies and leaving them breathless.

He held her for a moment longer, letting the intimacy wash over them, before sliding out and lying down next to her. He wrapped his arm around her and nestled his nose just beneath her ear. Her fingers traced patterns in his skin, lingering over freckles and scars, loving every part of him.

The moment spread before them, begging to be acknowledged. She didn't want to descend back into uncertainty, but she couldn't hide her honesty from him.

"That was unexpected," she said. "But pleasantly so."

He laughed, deep and throaty, and hugged her closer.

"Unexpected for you, maybe."

"What would you call it?"

"Inevitable."

She took in a deep breath. "Did you plan this?"

"No. But I've dreamed of it for so long. I wanted to try, even if you would say no."

How could he doubt, even for a moment, that she would accept him?

"I thought you wanted nothing to do with me," she admitted.

"I came back for you," he said.

"But why? Why me?"

He propped himself up on his elbow and lifted her chin to look into his eyes. He held her hand and kissed her fingers. "Because you," he kissed her hand again, "are amazing. You have been there for me even when I didn't deserve it." He started kissing her fingers one by one. "You fulfill me in ways nobody else can." He put her hand down and ran his fingers through her hair. "You are my muse. You are one of my favorite people ever. And I love you."

His confession had caught her off guard, but there was only one thing for her to say back to him. "I love you too."

ABOUT THE AUTHORS

C.W. Allen is a Midwestern transplant to rural Utah where she serves as the President-Elect of the League of Utah Writers. She writes long stories for children and short stories for former children. She is also a frequent guest presenter at writing conferences, which helps her procrastinate knuckling down to any actual writing. Her award-winning middle grade fantasy series *The Falinnheim Chronicles* is out now, with many more stories waiting in the wings. Follow her latest projects at cwallenbooks.com.

Lillian Angelovic writes award-winning poetry and fiction, and secretly edits every word she can get her hands on. She has a bachelor's degree in Broadcast Journalism, produces a popular faith-related leadership podcast, and helps recruit awesome people as hospital volunteers. Lillian lives in North Salt Lake, Utah, with her favorite movie partner, a crybaby cat, and a small forest of houseplants.

Meg Condie wishes she'd gone into piracy instead of college, but is trying to make the best of it by writing about adventures she hopes someday to have. When not washing dishes or doing laundry, she likes to read everything she can get ahold of, day dream, and play pretend with her toddlers.

Denis Feehan writes poetry and short stories, often with a humous bent. He is the President of Write On – St George, a writing group in Southern Utah. In his spare time, he is a musician and actor in Mesquite, NV.

G.R. Goodman is a retired vascular surgeon who is reorienting his right brain away from the art of medicine in new directions. Although he thinks there is nothing as poetic as a well sewn vascular anastomosis, he acknowledges that literary poetry appeals more to the collective heart of humanity. Continued learning and expansion into new horizons remain high on his life's list of goals.

Lorraine Jeffery's prose has appeared in many publications, including *Persimmon Tree, Focus on the Family, Elsewhere, Ocotillo, War Cry, Exponent II, Utah Senior Review* and *Mature Years*. She has published two books of poems: *When the Universe Brings Us Back* (2022) and Tethers (2023, Kelsay Books).

C. H. Lindsay (Charlie) is an award-winning poet, writer, housewife, and book-lover—not necessarily in that order. She currently has short stories and poems in over twenty anthologies (so far). Her poems have also appeared in magazines including *Amazing Stories, Fantasy Magazine, Space and Time, Strange Horizons,* and *The Leading Edge*. She is working on five novels, six short stories, and at least two dozen poems (although the numbers are always in flux). In 2018 she became Al Carlisle's literary executor. She now publishes his true crime under Carlisle Legacy Books, LLC. She is a member of SFWA, HWA, SFPA, LUW, and is a founding member of the Utah Chapter of the Horror Writers Association. Mostly blind, she lives in Utah with her "seeing-eye husband," library of books, and a bossy cat. You can learn more about her at www.chlindsay.net.

Terra Luft is an award-winning speculative fiction author whose imagination conjures mostly dark tales. Her work challenges readers to look at the world differently and explores adult themes, including what it means to be human. Terra holds a BA in Creative Writing and English with a minor in communications from Southern New Hampshire University and an MS in Management and Leadership from Western Governors University. She resides in the mountains of Utah with her husband and two daughters where she is most inspired to write when lost deep in the woods.

Margot Monroe lives in Salt Lake City with her husband, daughter, an Italian Greyhound, and a flock of black-capped chickadees and lesser goldfinches in her backyard. She's the North Central Liaison for the League of Utah Writers. You can find her writing romance at www.gowritemargot.com

Daniel Moreschi, a poet from Neath, South Wales, UK, encountered a profound turning point when his ongoing battle with severe M.E. upended his life. Nevertheless, it was during this period that he rediscovered his passion for poetry, which had lain dormant since his teenage years. Writing has since become a means of distraction from his struggles. Daniel has been acclaimed by many poetry competitions, including those hosted by The Oliver Goldsmith Literature Festival, Poets & Patrons, Wine Country Writers Festival, Short Stories Unlimited, Westmoreland Arts and Heritage Festival, The Hexham Poetry Prize, National Federation of State Poetry Societies, and Inchicore Ledwidge Society. His poetry has been published by The Society of Classical Poets, Black Cat Poetry Press, and The Lyric. Additionally, he has been nominated for both Best of the Net and the Pushcart Prize.

John M. Olsen edits and writes speculative fiction across multiple genres and loves stories about ordinary people stepping up to do extraordinary things. His short stories have appeared in dozens of anthologies. He's also written several novels across multiple genres, including the *Polecat Protocol* science fiction series (*Discovery, Breakdown, Emergence*), the *Riland Throne* fantasy series (*Crystal King, Crystal Queen, Crystal Empire*), and *High Hopes*, a historical military fantasy set in the JTF13 universe. He loves to create and fix things through editing and writing, just like when he's working in his secret lair equipped with dangerous power tools. In all cases, he applies engineering principles and processes to the task at hand, often in unpredictable ways. He lives in Utah with his lovely wife and a variable number of mostly grown children and a constantly changing subset of extended family and pets.

Pat Partridge writes fiction (both short stories and novels), humor, and occasional nonfiction. His book of political humor is in its third edition. He is the author of the mystery, *Fragile Memories*, and a sequel, *Vanishing Traces*, as well as a humorous road-trip novel, *Fast on Fifty*. He is the winner of several awards from the League of Utah Writers for his short fiction and novel first chapters over the past two years. Recently, his short fiction–some humorous, some the opposite–has appeared in *Remington Review, The Haven, Fabula Argentea, Ariel Chart, Litro,* and several anthologies. He is pleased others find his writing worth reading.

Rachael Bush published her fourth book, *Love on Location*, with The Wild Rose Press in 2018 under her pen name, September Roberts. As September, she writes romance that's smoking hot and always happy ever after. As Rachael, she writes the *Botany for Everyone* series, because everyone should know the basics of botany. You can find out more at botanyforeveryone.com. When she's not writing, she volunteers as the President of the League of Utah Writers, serves as the Blue Quill chapter president, and serves on the League's conference committee. For nerdy science and art, follow Rachael on Instagram @botanyforeveryone

M. Rohr enjoys reading and writing stories of all kinds, especially when her kids chime in with their ideas about what should happen. She lives along the Rocky Mountains, where she works from home while trying to prevent her two little hurricanes (read: toddlers) from destroying everything.

Talysa Sainz is a freelance editor and award-winning author who believes life's deepest truths can be found in fiction. She runs her own editing business and spends her time at the library or volunteering with the League of Utah Writers. Always fascinated with the structure of words, she studied English Linguistics and Editing at BYU. She then went on to receive a Master of Science in Management and Leadership, focusing on nonprofit work, from WGU. Talysa is the President of the Utah Freelance Editors.

Masha Shukovich (she/they) is a writer, storyteller, folklorist, neurodivergent person, and a brown immigrant from a country that no longer exists. Her ancestral and indigenous roots are in the Balkans; the Mediterranean; and West, Central and Northeast

Asia. Masha's awards include the 2022 Rick DeMarinis Short Story Award, 2022 Page Turner Mentorship Award, and the 2022 Courage to Write Writers of Note Award, among others. Masha's work was recently shortlisted for *The Masters Review's Anthology*; First Pages Prize; and Fractured Lit's Legends, Myths, & Allegories Prize. She is at work on a novel and a collection of short stories. Masha's writing is inspired by the lived experiences of people like themselves: humanimals, shapeshifters, and apparent outsiders who seem to belong nowhere and everywhere. Masha lives and writes on the land colonially known as the Salt Lake Valley and online at www.mashashukovich.com. Instagram: @mashawrites

Marie Tollstrup hails from a Wisconsin potato farm. In 1951 at fourteen, she entered a convent, the School Sisters of St. Francis, in Milwaukee. After graduating from Alverno College with a BA in English, she taught as a nun for ten years in Schiller Park and Wilmette in the Chicago area where she earned an MA in English from Loyola University. At Jordan High School in Long Beach, California, where she taught twenty-nine years, she founded and advised Stylus, a national award-winning literary/arts magazine for twenty-three years. In retirement, Marie focuses on poetry, but branches out to prose where she enters contests, winning awards for speaking her mind and poetic word play. Her poetry has been published in UTSPS's *Panorama* for ten years, in twelve League of Utah Writers' volumes, and in ASPS's *Sandcutters*. Read her published poems and prose in LUW's publications.

H.L. Voss is a queer and nonbinary author, poet, and lifelong learner. They are a computer science teacher by day, a writer by night, and neurodivergent all the time. When they aren't writing short stories or doing blackout poetry, they are trying to finish the manuscript that is currently plaguing their life. You can find them online at www.twitter.com/WriterHLVoss.

Monica J. Williams is a feminist writer with a Ph.D. in Sociology. An expert in gender, law, and society, Monica authored the book *The Sex Offender Housing Dilemma*, and has published numerous nonfiction essays and academic articles. She's currently working on a memoir in which she discovers joy and freedom in connecting to her body through meditative body scans, a practice that eventually leads her to leave her career in academia to live a more authentic life. Monica lives in Ogden, Utah. For more information on her projects and other writing, visit her website at www.monicajwilliams.com.

Bryan Young (he/they) works across many different media. His work as a writer and producer has been called "filmmaking gold" by The New York Times. He's also published comic books with Slave Labor Graphics and Image Comics. He's been a regular contributor for the *Huffington Post, StarWars.com, Star Wars Insider* magazine, SYFY, /Film, and was the founder and editor in chief of the geek news and review site *Big Shiny Robot*! In 2014, he wrote the critically acclaimed history book, *A Children's Illustrated History of Presidential Assassination*. He co-authored *Robotech: The Macross Saga RPG* has written two books in the BattleTech Universe: *Honor's Gauntlet* and *A Question of Survival*. His latest book, *The Big Bang Theory Book of Lists* is a #1 Bestseller on Amazon. His work has won two Diamond Quill awards and in 2023 he was named Writer of the Year by the League of Utah Writers. He teaches writing for Writer's Digest, Script Magazine, and at the University of Utah. Follow him across social media @swankmotron or visit swankmotron.com.

MORE FROM THE LEAGUE OF UTAH WRITERS

FIND ALL OUR ANTHOLOGIES AT LEAGUEOFUTAHWRITERS.COM

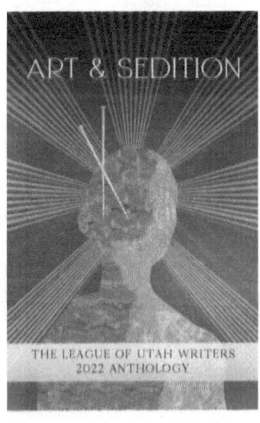

The League of Utah Writers   85th Anniversary Anthology

THE FUNCTION OF FREEDOM

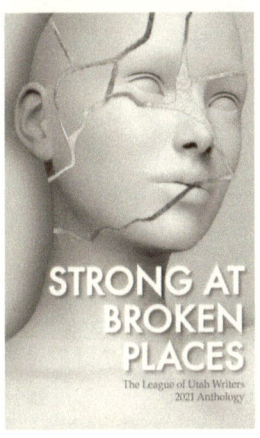

STRONG AT BROKEN PLACES

The League of Utah Writers
2021 Anthology

WHAT CAN THE LEAGUE OF UTAH WRITERS DO FOR YOU?

The League of Utah Writers is a non-profit organization dedicated to offering friendship, education, and encouragement to the writers and poets of Utah. Our organization aids our members in the improvement of their craft and support of their goals.

The League of Utah Writers is a vibrant writing community with chapters throughout the state, as well as online with members across the country. Membership in the League of Utah Writers provides support and opportunities for writers and editors at all levels of their careers.

Join us at www.leagueofutahwriters.com

The Pre-Quill Conference

Pre-Quill is the League of Utah Writers' Spring writing conference - a day long event of classes, workshops, and networking with other wordsmiths.

This event showcases our local Utah writers in classes and courses geared to each unique voice and talent. It is also a great place to start working on stories, poetry, or any of the other categories listed in the Wooley awards - the League's prestigious contest awarded at the annual Quills conference each year.

Pre-Quill helps refresh your creative neurons with the pulse and energy only spring could bring.

Find more about The Pre-Quill Conference at
www.leagueofutahwriters.com

T H E
QUILLS
CONFERENCE

The League of Utah Writers invites you to join us for the Quills Conference, hosted locally in Salt Lake City annually near the end of summer.

The Quills Conference is the League's premium event, bringing in special guest authors, agents, editors, and publishers from around the nation.

This four-day writing conference is for everyone from the fresh voices not yet published to the well-established writers seeking to make a difference in their writing community.

The Quills Conference's annual banquet is also home to The Woolley Awards writing contest and the Quill Awards for published works.

Find out more about Quills at
www.leagueofutahwriters.com